I0566966

Inaccurate Realities
A Young Adult Speculative Fiction Magazine

Volume 6

Love

Inaccurate Realities: A Young Adult Speculative Fiction Magazine
www.inaccuraterealities.com
Volume Six

Editor: Christa J Seeley
Assistant Editors: Andrea Modolo, Sara Eagleson
Proofreader: Danielle Webster
Cover Art: Sara Eagleson
Social Media: Jaaron Collins
Image Credits: Canstock photos csp22310475, csp22107393

Inaccurate Realities is a quarterly magazine.
Published out of Gatineau, Quebec.

Contributor guidelines for writers and artists are available on our
website or can be requested through:
submission.inaccuraterealities@gmail.com

Table of Contents

Love

Gnat and Sixty-Two
Valerie Hunter

For the eightieth time in the past two weeks, Kate wondered what in heaven's name she'd done.

The steam balloon loomed in front of her, a shimmery shadow in the darkness, and though Captain Nobile had repeatedly called the balloons "petite carriers" during their training, this thing looked anything but petite.

She breathed deeply and kept walking toward it. She was just the passenger. The pilot knew what he was doing. Focus on the mission.

When that didn't do much to quiet the jangling in her brain, she reminded herself that she'd chosen this. Excitement. Escape. A way out of the orphanage that didn't involve becoming someone's maid.

But that wishful Kate felt like some other person, some person she'd left behind two weeks ago. She was in the army now. Well, sort of. She wasn't the same person.

Heck, she wasn't even a girl anymore, at least as far as anyone around her was concerned.

She was two feet from the balloon when a voice came from the dark, "You Courier Sixty-two?"

"Yessir," she said quickly. She could just make out his silhouette next to the balloon, thin and slouchy.

"The *sir's* not necessary. It's just Nat. Let's get a shake on. You ever been up in a balloon?"

"No." She eyed the side of the balloon, hoping to see some kind of door or step.

"You hop over," Nat said, doing so in one quick motion that didn't give her any better idea of how to do it. "Use the edge of the basket, it's sturdy."

She managed to get in, flopping and landing in a heap in the bottom. She was glad for the dark; she couldn't see Nat's face and he couldn't see hers. She could make out the dim shapes of the basket's contents, and she repeated them in her head. She'd studied the diagrams; it was comforting to know what everything was—the console with its luminescent levers and buttons, the enormous fuel tank in the middle, a seat to the left, the stow box next to that which held the emergency supplies: blankets, a med kit, a gun.

"Come on, have a seat. Let's get on with it."

She hurried to the seat, and Nat set levers on the console and then pulled in the tethers. They were up. She felt it in her stomach and closed her eyes, but that only made the feeling worse. So she opened them again, kept her eyes on the silhouette of Nat's back, tried to steady herself.

Nat turned from the console. "You doing all right?"

"It's smoother than I thought it'd be." Her voice seemed small in the vast dark sky.

He grinned, a flash of white teeth. She wished he'd keep his eyes on where he was going, but she couldn't very well tell him that.

"Once you get used to it—next time, maybe—you should try standing up. Better view."

If she stood up she might look down, which she had no desire to do, but she nodded anyway. Nat turned back toward the sky, but he kept talking. "You from around here?"

They'd been instructed not to talk to the pilot, not to distract him, but it would be rude not to answer. "The county orphanage."

"Ah. Looking for adventure?"

"Something like that."

"You're a girl, aren't you?"

He might have well have punched her in the gut. "How'd you know?"

"I didn't, not for sure, till you just told me. You've got to try harder than that, Sixty-two. Someone says you're a girl, you deny it. Act offended. Most likely they'll feel bad for being wrong."

She tried to right her tilting mind. She was used to lessons taking place in Captain Nobile's big tent, surrounded by the other couriers. She'd always been good at lessons.

"What if they don't?" she asked. "What if they still think I'm a girl?"

He threw another flash of teeth over his shoulder. "Offer to show 'em you're not."

Her horror crept to her cheeks in a hot blush. "But I couldn't . . . I mean . . . "

Nat grinned bigger. "No one's going to take you up on it. Probably not, anyway."

"There's too many *probably*'s and *maybe*'s in your figuring."

"Ah, that's what being a courier is. Uncertainty. Probably you'll never get caught. Most likely no one will ever notice you. But you never know. It helps to consider the possibilities."

The possibilities gave her a hollow spot in the pit of her stomach that made her want to puke. She'd been doing her best *not* to think about them, but maybe Nat knew best. Maybe if you thought about the scary things enough, they ceased to be scary.

"So what made you think I might be a girl?" she asked.

She expected him to say something about the pitch of her voice or her size, but instead he said, "You slouch too much."

"What? Boys slouch! You're slouching right now."

He snorted. "You're trying to pass for what? A thirteen-, fourteen-year-old boy? Boys that age want to be seen as men. And if they're as small as you, they want to take advantage of every inch they've got."

She straightened her posture. "Better?"

"Better, but try not to look like someone's ramming a poker up your spine."

"You said to stand straight!"

"I said not to slouch. There's a difference. Haven't you ever watched a thirteen-year-old boy walk?"

"I can't say that's a subject they taught me in school," she snapped.

"Well, start observing," he said, his tone equally sharp.

"I fooled Captain Nobile," she said. "And the recruitment officer, and all the boys in my tent. I reckon I'm good enough."

"Your job is to be perfect, not 'good enough.' 'Good enough' is what's going to get you killed."

His words dropped like sticks of dynamite into that little pit in her stomach, blowing it wide open.

She swallowed. "Do a lot of couriers die?" she asked, and beneath her fear she felt a tiny kernel of pride that she could still keep her voice calm and steady.

"Enough," he said. "They didn't tell you that at the recruitment, did they?"

"No," she said. Would it have mattered if they had? How dire of a warning would it have taken?

Nat had turned back to the balloon's control panel. "What you've got to do," he said, his voice relaxed again, "is pack that fear away somewhere. Don't lose it, but don't take it out and play with it either. Just try to be whoever it is you're supposed to be."

Tommy Knight. That was the name they'd given her, the name she wasn't supposed to tell Nat, the name she hoped she'd never have to use, because if no one asked who she was, it meant she was doing her job successfully.

She was acquiring too many names. Tommy Knight. Courier Sixty-two. Leon Ackerman, which was the name she'd given the recruitment officer. Kate felt far away, lost under everyone else.

"Are you allowed to know my real name?" she asked.

He shot her a look over his shoulder. "Did you listen to a word of your orientation, Courier Sixty-two?"

"I don't mean my courier alias, or even the name I gave the army. I mean my real name. My girl name."

"No."

"Please?" she asked, the word slipping from her mouth before she could help it.

"Code seventeen point two: an aeronaut should not know the name of his courier in case he is captured and tortured for information."

"You know I'm a girl," she pointed out. "That seems like far more helpful information you might give up under torture."

"Well, no one ever said the army made much sense. But I don't want to know your name."

"But I know your name. Your first name, anyway."

He laughed. "It's a nickname."

"Well, yes, I figured that. Nathaniel? Nathan?"

"Not that kind of nickname."

"What do you mean?"

"The couriers get numbers. The aeronauts get called after flying things. Birds, mostly."

"I never heard of a Nat bird."

"All the good bird names were taken when I came along. So they called me Gnat. Like the bug."

She laughed before considering if she should. Gnats were so . . . inconsequential. Annoying. She'd only known him twenty minutes, but neither adjective seemed to fit Nat. Gnat.

"So anyway that's all the names we need. Gnat and Sixty-two. All right?"

It wasn't, not really, but she couldn't very well argue with him. "All right. But if I'm about to die, I'm telling you my name. Someone ought to know."

He didn't answer, and they flew in silence after that. The sky seemed slightly less black, and she went through the steps of her mission. They would land a mile from the message site. She would walk there—it was a blacksmith's forge—and ask for a penny's worth of horseshoe nails. She'd receive them, along with the message, which she'd slip into the hidden inner pocket of her coat. Walk away, innocent as pie, and make her calm and careful way back to the balloon. If for whatever reason the balloon was gone, she was to continue walking north, just a young traveler on the road, keeping an eye out for a balloon that might come for her, eventually.

Easy.

The balloon touched down with the sun still not up, which was the intent; they flew at night to be less visible. But she was supposed to wait till sunrise to leave it, because she couldn't very well see in the dark.

The horizon turned a hazy purple. She stood up, legs shaky. She still couldn't see Gnat clearly, but his silhouette seemed to exude calmness.

She wondered which of them had the more dangerous job. Once she left the balloon, she would be an innocent, nameless boy, unlikely to be noticed by anyone, whereas he would continue to sit in the balloon, hidden somewhat by the grove of trees in front of them, but visible from the other direction, or by anyone who happened to come through the trees, or—

Of course, being in the balloon meant he had a vehicle of escape, too. Unlike her.

The sky took on new shades, the shadows receding. "Get on with it, Sixty-two."

She nodded once and climbed out of the balloon, making less of a hash of it than when she'd gotten in.

"You're thinking too much," he said.

She stopped, turned back to him. "I'm not supposed to think?"

"You're not supposed to *show* you're thinking. You're just a kid out for a walk, remember? A simple errand."

She nodded, trying to relax her face, her shoulders. Trying to become Tommy Knight.

By the time she reached the forge, she thought she'd more or less succeeded in looking relaxed and innocent, though of course there was no one to ask. She felt like she had a bellyful of grasshoppers, but she ignored that, asking the blacksmith for a penny's worth of horseshoe nails and giving him the two-headed penny that was supposed to serve as her signal. He barely glanced at the coin, and for a moment she wondered what she was supposed to do if all she got in return was the nails, but no, there was a little slip of paper along with the sack. She put it in her secret pocket as quickly as possible—she'd practiced the move dozens of times in the courier tent—and walked away.

Her ability to be innocent Tommy Knight slipped away on her

way back, now that she had the message. It took every ounce of her control not to look wildly around for someone who might be following her, not to run, not to stop and puke.

But she made it back, and the balloon was still there, Gnat somehow managing to look both alert and bored as he peered out of it. He nodded to her, and she climbed in with something approaching ease.

She could see him now in the full light. A young man with crooked shoulders and dark hair. As he moved to get the tethers up, she noticed he limped.

"Easy, right?" he said as they ascended.

"I guess," she mumbled.

"No guesses about it. Have some confidence. Just don't be confident."

"That doesn't make any sense."

He laughed. "That's life, Sixty-two. Especially this life. Contradictions at every turn."

❧

It was a weird life, but she started to get acclimated to it. Each run—there were usually two a week—seemed a little more normal, and if she didn't feel exactly confident, at least she felt a little more like Tommy Knight each time.

Gnat was a helpful part of that process. In camp she kept to herself, afraid that if she talked too much one of the other couriers would realize she was a girl. Gnat already knew, didn't seem to care, and was generally chatty, which made their journeys less nerve-wracking than they might have been.

She got to the point where she didn't mind standing up during the flight, didn't even mind looking down. Everything looked so small from above, so inconsequential yet beautiful. She had a certain dread of missions, but never of the flights.

"You ever milk a cow?" she asked on their fifth mission, as they passed over a field of them on their way back to camp.

He gave her a look like she was crazy. "No."

"Me either. Someday I'd like to."

He laughed. "You've got some nice dreams there, Sixty-two."

"Don't you ever think about what you want to do after the war?"

"Keep flying. I've got money saved up for a balloon of my own."

"Don't you want a real home?"

"The sky's a real enough home for me. When I'm up here . . . it's like I never want to go down, you know? It's just so beautiful."

She could hear the love for it in his voice, and she smiled. "Well, I'd like an on-the-ground home. My own farm. My own cows. They're giving free land out in the Territories, did you know that?"

"Not to the likes of us," he said.

"What do you mean?"

"You have to be twenty-one to claim land."

She hadn't known that, but it was the "us" that gave her pause. "You have to be twenty-one to be an aeronaut, too."

"Government's fond of bending the rules when it suits them. We both know that, eh?"

She'd never stopped to consider how old Gnat was before. She'd put him in the category labeled "grown," and left it at that. Now she looked at him more closely. "You're not twenty-one?"

At first she thought he wasn't going to respond, was going to hold on to his age like he did his name, but then he said, "I'm eighteen."

She had to bite her lip to keep from gawping at him. Just two years older than her, and here she'd been trusting him this whole time like he was an adult. "How long have you been an aeronaut?"

"Little over a year. I don't have my official certs, but that doesn't seem to bother anyone. Army needs pilots. I was a courier first, learned to fly from my pilot. When he died, I took over."

Gnat's eyes were back on the horizon, his jaw set and twitchy, the way the little boys at the orphanage got when they were trying not to cry. He didn't look grown anymore.

"You were really a courier?" she asked.

He managed a small smile. "Don't sound so shocked. Where do you think all my good advice comes from? I was a little older than most, but the limp made up for that. No one ever suspects a cripple's up to anything."

"You're not a—"

"Sure I am. But it was a benefit as a courier, and it doesn't matter none in the sky."

She tried to juggle this new information, slot it together like a puzzle. "Do you . . . Do you ever regret it? Becoming a courier? A pilot?" He still didn't look at her. "Wasn't much else for me to do."

"Me neither," she said, keeping her eyes on the clouds. "I could have gone to work as a maid, but . . . I wanted to see a little of the world, you know? Is that a stupid reason for joining the couriers?"

"No stupider than most. Less stupid than some. At least you don't want to be a hero. I ever tell you about the courier I had before you? Fifty-nine?"

"No."

"That boy had a pure love for his country. Wanted to be a hero. Didn't end well for him."

She'd never thought much about Gnat's previous courier, what had happened to him. She didn't want to ask. She still didn't. But she said, "We're in the army. Aren't we supposed to love our country?"

"Do you?"

"Well, I never really thought about it . . . "

"That means you don't," Gnat said. "We respect our country. We want to do right by it. I certainly hope we win the war, and I'll do what I can to make that happen. But if it comes to a choice between myself and my country, I'm looking out for my own hide first. You'd do best to do the same.

"Courier Fifty-nine, now, he put his country first. All he ever talked about was being a hero. I guess that's noble, but it doesn't make him any less dead."

"How'd he die?" she asked, even though she still didn't want to know.

"Got himself shot 'bout twenty feet from the balloon. Reb officer was chasing him, telling him to halt. Fifty-nine should have listened, should have played innocent. He had a very innocent face, he probably could've pulled it off. Or maybe he couldn't have, and he would've gone to Confed prison. Either way he could've lived. But Fifty-nine thought he could be a hero, make it back to the balloon with the message. And instead he got himself killed and didn't deliver his message. Not wise. Never try to be a hero, Sixty-two."

It sounded more like fear than heroics to her. She could picture it all too clearly, the mad dash back to the balloon, the panic of trying to think fast, make the right decision. Maybe Fifty-nine figured he was dead either way. She doubted he wanted to be a hero right then. But she didn't try to explain that to Gnat. Instead she asked, "What did you do when he got shot?"

"I did what I was supposed to do. I left."

"How do you know he was for certain dead, then?"

"He got shot in the head."

"Oh." She could easily picture everything through Fifty-nine's eyes. The panicked running. The devastation of watching the balloon leave without him. She knew it was protocol, knew Gnat would do the same to her if it came to that. She wouldn't blame him, not one bit, but that wouldn't make it any less awful if it happened.

On the ground, life in camp wasn't so different than the orphanage. She was quiet. A cog in the machine. A nonentity.

In the sky it was different. She had a voice up there, and it was easy to dream. "Do you know if girls can claim land out in the Territories?" she asked Gnat one day.

"Probably not."

She didn't allow herself to be disappointed. "You think I could pass for a twenty-one-year-old man?"

"Not unless you grow a few inches. And grow some whiskers. Why do you want this farm so bad, anyway?"

She tried to find the words to explain it, but nothing seemed quite right. "It would be mine," she said finally.

He made a face, a little twist of his mouth that said her answer wasn't good enough.

"What?" she demanded. "You want a balloon of your own, don't you? It's the same thing."

"I want a balloon because I love flying. Do you love farming?"

"I don't know yet. I could. I was good in the orphanage garden."

He pulled another face. "You can't just make yourself love something. You can't just make a home."

"Why not?"

His eyes were on some far spot on the horizon. "A home's not a place. I lived in a house, when I was young, and it was never home. A home's where you feel . . . most yourself. Feel most comfortable. Most . . . "

"I could feel that way on a farm," she argued when he didn't go on.

He sighed like she was being dense, but then he said, "Well, maybe you could. Lord knows I never expected to find a home up here."

"How long did it take you to feel that way?" she asked. "How long before flying felt like home and not . . . I don't know, really scary?"

"It's never scary."

"Don't you worry about crashing?"

"Why would I crash?"

"Something could go wrong. You could get shot down."

"Things can go wrong on the ground, too."

She wanted to say that things going wrong on the ground didn't involve plummeting thousands of feet, but she held her tongue. His confidence was kind of endearing.

"It's just knowing what to do," he said, like it was the simplest thing in the world. "I can't do much, but I can be a damn good aeronaut." He paused. "You could be, too."

"What, an aeronaut? There aren't any girl pilots."

He laughed. "There aren't any girl couriers, but that doesn't seem to be stopping you. What the army doesn't know won't hurt them, and the sky doesn't care. You want to give it a try?"

She'd never thought of being an aeronaut before, but the way he presented the idea, like it was the most natural thing in the world, made her feel warm inside. Full of purpose.

"Sure," she said, and joined him at the console.

❤

In some ways learning to pilot the balloon was simple, or at least logical. She learned what each of the instruments did, how to read the gauges and meters, what to press or pull when. Other aspects were more difficult—the variables of wind and weather, the feelings you had to watch for when something just wasn't right. Gnat called it the difference between knowing how to be an aeronaut and knowing how to fly.

"It's just experience," he said. "Of course you can't get too confident. The sky is forever unpredictable."

"Sounds like being a courier."

"Exactly. If you can do one, you can do the other. You're going to be a fine aeronaut, Sixty-two."

The missions became secondary—she was still careful about them, of course, but she didn't fear them. They just had to be gotten through. After a couple months Gnat started to let her fly on her own during their runs, talking her through the tricky bits and only relieving her when they landed back at camp, so no one would see.

"Pretty soon you won't even need me," he said after a particularly sweet landing at their site. "I'm just here to watch the balloon while you go on your mission."

She wanted to tell him that she did need him, that his presence in the balloon was what kept her calm, but she couldn't seem to find the words. So she just said, "Make sure you take good care of it while I'm gone."

"Will do."

It was a mission like any other, at a farm outside of town. She stopped to talk to the farmer, asking for a job, and he apologized that he didn't have any work for her. He shook her hand and passed her the message.

She didn't know when she was first aware of being followed on her way back, but she didn't turn around, didn't break stride. She kept her pace the same—steady but not urgent—even as her mind raced.

She should switch direction. Not lead whoever it was to the balloon. Except she'd have to do it subtle-like, and she was running out of space. The balloon was already visible, if you knew what you were looking for. If her follower had spotted it, that might be his objective, and Gnat was in danger.

She told herself it wasn't her job to warn him. Her first priority was to protect the message, and his was to the balloon. She knew that, but it felt all wrong. Gnat was more important than any slip of paper.

She veered ever so gently to the left, a path that would take her parallel to the balloon rather than straight to it. Likely Gnat was watching, could see the threat and would take off. That was what he *should* do.

She didn't dare look in the direction of the balloon, but the lack of movement in her peripheral vision told her he was staying put. Not good. If he wasn't doing what he was supposed to, what was *she* supposed to do?

Protocol seemed to have left her. All she could hear in her head was Gnat's voice, mocking Fifty-nine and telling her not to be a hero.

When she got a few feet past the balloon, she took a sharp right away from it. As she had planned, it gave her a look at her follower.

A Confed lieutenant.

She didn't have time to think what to do next. His gun was already levelled at her chest.

"Where you going, sonny?" he asked in a perfectly pleasant tone.

She put her hands up, because surely that was what Tommy Knight would do. Just taking a walk, and stopped by a Confed soldier! It was a thrilling adventure.

"Walking down to the river." She tried to achieve the right amount of fear and awe in her voice. No guilt.

The lieutenant's eyes never left hers. "Don't lie to me, boy. What do you know about that balloon over there?"

She turned to look at it, letting her mouth hang open because this was Tommy Knight's first time seeing a balloon so close, and wasn't it a sight to behold? She kept her own self hidden behind Tommy's wide eyes, looking for Gnat. She couldn't see him.

"Is that one of them spy balloons?" she whispered to the lieutenant, letting the awe spill out in great gushes.

"Don't play dumb, kid." She thought she could hear just a hint of doubt in his voice, but before she could get too hopeful, his hand clamped on her shoulder.

"What do you mean?" she whined. Keep acting innocent, but don't do anything stupid. She repeated this to herself, for all the good it did her. All that protocol studied, and there was nothing to let her know what to do at this very moment.

The lieutenant didn't seem to know what to do, either. His fingers stayed like a vice on her arm, but his eyes were on the balloon. If Gnat took off now, he'd get shot down. But if the lieutenant had to take her back to . . . wherever he was going to take her, Gnat might escape in the meantime.

Apparently the lieutenant was thinking the same thing, because he raised his gun again and dragged her closer to the balloon.

"What are we doing?" she asked with the innocence of Tommy Knight, her stomach a clenched fist.

"Shut your mouth," the lieutenant growled, his fingers biting deeper into the meat of her shoulder.

And then there was a flash of movement to the left of the balloon, and she registered it was Gnat at the same time she heard the gunshot, the loudness of it so all-consuming as the lieutenant fell away behind her and Gnat staggered but didn't fall, and then he was dragging her and shoving her at the balloon, and everything was just happening, time no longer a linear thing but a great confusing lump.

The lieutenant still gripped her shoulder, she could feel his fingers, yet she was in the balloon and the lieutenant was on the ground, his hands scrabbling against the dirt in the most terrible way. There was a white, snowy silence muffling her ears, yet she could hear a thousand sounds—the lieutenant screaming, Gnat's voice (though she couldn't discern the words), and then soldiers streaming through the trees—thirteen or three, she couldn't be sure—and there were more shots, an *oomph* of breath from Gnat as he staggered against the console, and they were up, though the balloon lurched crazily, injured like Gnat though she couldn't see the wound.

The sky made it easier to think, though her head was still awhirl. "You all right?" Gnat asked, his voice soft and scared.

She looked herself up and down to be sure. "Yes. You?"

"I'm fine." His voice sounded stronger, more normal, so she was halfway to believing him. "We nicked the fuel line, though. Get over here and fly while I try to fix it."

She took his place at the console, staring at the wildly waving arrow on the fuel gauge, the smear of blood on the altimeter. She looked over at Gnat.

"Eyes on the sky, Sixty-two," he said, and she obeyed.

She heard him swear, a long string of words more tired than angry, and then he said, "Get us some altitude. We're right over a damn Confed camp."

She didn't look down, just pulled the acel lever and brought them up high while her stomach plummeted to some unknown depth. The balloon wobbled like a drunk, but it kept going. Below she heard the deep rumble of a cannon, but they were already out of range.

"You shouldn't have done that," she said, the high altitude making her feel breathless and hysterical. "You should have left me there. Protocol—"

"It was too late to leave by the time I spotted him. I was trying to save my own damn skin."

She couldn't tell if he was lying.

"Got it patched," Gnat said. "How's the fuel gauge looking?"

The arrow eased into place. "One gallon."

"That'll have to do. Bring her down a little, and pull on steady-like."

"You don't want to take over?" she asked.

"Nah, you're doing fine."

She snuck a look at him as he staggered over to the stow box, leaving a trail of blood behind him. When he saw her looking, he said, "Eyes on the sky."

"You look at me all the time when you're flying," she protested.

"Not when I'm making a tricky getaway with low fuel. Focus, Sixty-two."

She turned her gaze back to the sky. "How bad are you hurt?"

"Not bad. I'm just a little light headed."

He'd taken a seat, and was getting the med kit from the stow box. She could see blood on his hands, but with his dark coat and trousers, she couldn't tell where it was coming from.

"Eyes," he growled at her again.

"How many times were you hit?"

He paused too long before saying, "Once." She'd seen him get hit at least twice, and now she wondered if it wasn't three times or more, because why bother lying for a difference of one? Oh, god—

She tried to sort out the jumble of time in her head into something coherent. Something helpful. The lieutenant had shot Gnat when Gnat had shot him. She had seen Gnat stagger backwards and then right himself and grab her. That couldn't have been so bad, could it? Upper shoulder, maybe, or arm. If it had been too bad, he would've collapsed right away, like the lieutenant. And after that? Where else had he been hit?

She glanced at him again, wanting to go to him but knowing she couldn't let go of the acel lever and drift, not when they were so low on fuel. He had turned his back to her, so she couldn't see what he was doing.

"Why don't we land at the next town?" she suggested. "Refuel, and find you a doctor."

"I'm all right."

"You're bleeding."

"It's not that bad. We've got a mission to finish."

"What happened to 'don't be a hero'?"

"I'm not being a hero, I'm being smart. It's too dangerous to just land. Could be a Confed presence. Just steady on to our camp, all right?"

She kept going. Endless minutes of flying, of her eyes darting from the sky to the fuel gauge to Gnat. Should she try to rig something up to keep a steady pull on the acel lever, so she could go to him? What if they ran out of fuel? What if she botched their landing?

"Maybe you should land," she suggested.

"You'll be all right." His voice sounded confident, strong. Maybe he wasn't doing so bad after all.

Before she could fully enjoy her relief, the fuel gauge needle landed on zero, and the balloon bucked like a recalcitrant horse, no longer in her control. She was thrown into the console, the lurch going through her whole body like a jolt of lightning. Behind her, Gnat screamed in pain.

"Gnat!" she yelled, twisting to look at him. He attempted to get up, but landed back in the seat, his face grey, and that was when true panic set in, because she could deal with the balloon crashing, but not with him dying, not with—

"It's all right," he said, soft but audible, and her heart started beating again. "You've got about two minutes before it goes into freefall. Ease the valve line down, and release the acel lever. Nice and easy."

"I can't," she said, even as she did it. The balloon descended slowly, tilting a bit but not running away.

"You've got it," he said, and he sounded calm, like he really believed in her. "Just keep doing that. And look at the sky, Sixty-two. Isn't it beautiful?"

It was. Pure blue. Vast and glorious. You couldn't crash from a sky like that. You couldn't die.

"You're a natural born pilot."

"I have a good teacher," she said. She knew what he meant now, about being at home in the sky. Here she was plummeting out of it, but she'd never felt so in love, so full of the sunset, and the balloon, and the feeling of flying.

So full of Gnat.

"One last thing to do," Gnat said from behind her, his voice still steady. "Pull the drift lever, and brace yourself against the console. Landing's probably going to be bumpy."

She pulled, and the balloon lurched, rolled—oh, god, she was going to kill them both after all—and then hit the ground as gently as a raindrop. She stood still, waiting for the realization that they were still in the sky, but no, she had really landed, landed perfectly, with the camp a haze of shadows on the horizon.

A laugh burst from her lips, an amazed, slightly hysterical laugh that came from somewhere deep inside, somewhere that wasn't Courier Sixty-two or Tommy Knight or Leon Ackerman, somewhere that was pure Kate.

"I did it."

She turned to Gnat, and he was smiling at her, but her happiness evaporated. He was so pale. They weren't in the sky anymore, and the ground meant reality, and all that blood, and not knowing what to do.

She was beside him in an instant, tugging open his jacket and staring at all the blood on his shirt, holes in his shoulder and chest, another in his leg.

"It's all right," she said, repeating it as she tried to plug him up. Despite the panic in her voice, she half believed her own words; he couldn't die, not after that beautiful sky, that perfect landing. Not when she felt so full of love for him.

"It's all right. It's all right, Gnat."

His eyes were closed, but his lips were moving, struggling to say something, and she bent close.

"It's James," he whispered, and then he was silent.

❧

Later it was just as much of a blur as when they'd taken off, escaping the Rebs. She had ascertained that he was still breathing, tucked the blanket from the stow box tight around him, and took off running toward their camp, ignoring the pain in her chest where she'd cracked her ribs against the console, ignoring everything but her mission. Nothing had mattered except getting Gnat back to camp, getting him to a doctor, keeping him alive.

She'd done it, somehow, and then she'd passed out.

She woke up to find herself in an unfamiliar bed with Captain Nobile standing above her.

"Sir," she managed to mumble.

He nodded at her.

"What happened?"

"You broke some ribs. Possible concussion. The doctor thinks you should spend a while in bed."

She just looked at him, the events coming back to her slowly: the shots, the blood, landing the balloon. Gnat.

"Is Gnat…"

"Lost his leg, and a lot of blood. He's holding his own, though. Seems you were a big help in that. Pity we can't keep you on."

"Sir?" she said, trying to hold onto her disguise till the end, even as her mind was on Gnat.

"Can't have a girl in the courier service," he said, sounding almost apologetic.

She nearly denied it, but of course the doctor had examined her. So she just nodded. This life had ended. She needed to figure out how to be Kate again.

It wasn't an easy task, particularly not in this strange bed, left alone except for the doctor's visits. Her head hurt and her chest hurt, but when she closed her eyes she could pretend she was in the sky with Gnat and a head full of dreams. The more she thought about them, the more she sorted through them, the less impossible they seemed. He'd given her a home in his balloon. He'd tried to tell her a home wasnt a place, and she understood now. She understood.

It was four days before the doctor would let her out of bed, another two before she was allowed to see Gnat. Plenty of time for dreaming, for planning.

Gnat looked awful. Pale, with dark hollows beneath his eyes. He looked small, too, bundled in the bed, a strange depression in the sheets where his leg should have been. She felt suddenly shy. This was James and not Gnat. She didn't know James.

"Sixty-two," he said quietly. "You all right?"

She nodded, sitting down beside his bed. "How are you feeling?"

He gave a huff of breath that wasn't quite a laugh. "I've been better."

"I'm sorry," she said.

He wasn't looking at her. "Captain Nobile came by yesterday. Relieved me of my post. Said I was never flying again."

"Never flying for the *army* again," she corrected. "Which is not such a terrible thing, is it?"

But Gnat's eyes looked wet. "It was my good leg."

She reached for his hand tentatively, found it and gripped it tight. "You'll be all right. You'll get one of those gadgety legs, and you can fly wherever you want, no more courier runs or getting shot at—"

"With what balloon?" he demanded, voice ragged.

"We'll find one," she said. "They kicked me out, too, did I mention? We're both free. You said you have money saved, and I have my pay, too . . . " She paused, not sure if she ought to go on. But why shouldn't she? She was done with not saying things. "We'll get a balloon and fly out west . . . "

He frowned. "Get a farm, too?"

"Sure. I don't think I can pass for a twenty-one year old man, but you can."

He shook his head. "What cloud are you living on? Dreams aren't that easy. I'm a crippled aeronaut who probably can't fly anymore, and you . . . Well, you don't need me."

She stared at him. Maybe he'd been Gnat—and whatever courier number he'd been before that—for so long that he'd forgotten how to be James. Forgotten how to be a person and not a job.

Except he hadn't. She needed to remind him of that. "You waited for me, didn't you?" she asked. "You could have left, gotten away, but you waited. You shot that officer to rescue me."

He still wasn't looking at her, but he nodded.

"Well, I could probably fly out there myself if I had to. And maybe I could even get the land myself, too, with the right disguise. But I need you to make it a home. I need you."

He looked at her now, but his eyes were unreadable.

"You're my best friend. I love you," she supplied, in case he really didn't get it. "Say you'll come with me."

He kept looking at her for a long moment. "You really think you can fly out there on your own, huh?"

She laughed. "I seem to recall someone telling me I was a good pilot. Although I might need you to talk me through my landings."

A smile twitched the ends of his mouth. "I could maybe handle that. I don't think I'll be much help farming, though."

"You don't need to be. I'll do the farming. Or we'll open our own courier business, and use the money to hire help."

"You've got all this planned out, don't you, Sixty-two?"

"It's Kate," she said. "And I do."

"Plans don't mean much, Kate."

"Maybe not. And I'm sure this one won't go perfectly. But we'll be all right. You haven't been outside today, but I have. The sky's beautiful. And it's ours."

The Necromancer's Apprentice
K D Callaghan

The box was gritty as I took it from the delivery boy, covered in dust from the desert. Glyphs etched on the black lid brushed with red sand. It was a toss-up as to which was grittier, my eyes or the box.

"Thank you," I said, yawning. Balancing the box on one arm I dug into my robes with the other. His eyes went wide when I offered him a silver coin. Dark fingers—darker than mine—snatched it out of my hand faster than a silverfish swimming downstream as he bowed.

"Ancestors bless you, Apprentice," he said, already turning back to his wagon and his horses, eager not just to get away, but away from me. The Yallora don't like Necromancers; it doesn't matter that I'm half-Yallora and only a lowly apprentice stuck on delivery duty. They whisper about our powers, say that we tread where no one should ever go, disturbing ancestors and spirits, unbalancing the land as we raise and dance with the dead. One glimpse of my robes and they believe I can curse and condemn them in half a thought, even though that's the farthest thing from the truth.

In truth, delivery detail is a step up for me and a sign that the temple superiors might finally be ready to let me re-take my Spectrolite test. They are trusting me with our water stones after all.

That said, I'm still the furthest behind in my year, barely able to do the most basic of regulations and stone rituals. But the delivery boy doesn't know that, and so he headed away from the city as fast as he could; back out into the desert, where the bushes fade to scrubby, patchy grass and red soil turns white under the heat of the sun.

I sighed, heading for the shade of the nearest merchant stall. Why did deliveries have to happen so early? Years ago I would have been up already, rising with my father for the morning tide, but now rising early was painful. The sun was barely a hand's span above the horizon and we went to bed *late*. Late enough that the few people out this early were giving me strange looks. The other apprentices mentioned it, but I wouldn't have noticed—people look at me strangely all the time because of my skin. I moved under the shade of the stone merchant's embroidered canopy to inspect the box.

The polished wood table gleamed. Few can afford the ebon wood from the southeast islands and fewer still actually use it, but as he's the only merchant in the city who can guarantee us the quantity of water stones we need he's quite rich. They're integral to most of the soul-mending and spirit-healing rituals we perform; they open pathways, soothe wounds of the heart and mind, and are the best stone for balancing emotional energies.

Brushing sand off the runes on top of the box, I pressed down on the latch, metal cool under the pads of my fingers as it sprang open. That was a good sign; warm metal meant spoiled or fake stones. Three small pouches lay inside, hide etched with marks in ash, shimmering slightly as I opened them and examined the nine glassy blue stones.

Even completely dry, water stones feel wet—not slimy, but ever so slightly damp, like they've been dipped in dew. Only the Yallora shamans know where to find them and how to contain them. Rumour has them forming a thousand different ways—in the blooms of cacti after a desert rain, in the heart of an oasis, some even say they're spheres of stone, seeped in moistures, harvested from deep inside caves buried under the sand.

To the Yallora, my mother's people, they are sacred. A source of reverence and healing and life. Souls of ancestors fallen from the sky to help heal the land. Desert tribes have been trading them with coastal tribes for eons; enriching the people enriches the land. To the pale-skinned Rigauls, my father's kin, they're a tool. A mystic one, but still a tool.

I held a stone up to the light, looking for the characteristic waves, like light streaming through water. Seeing them, I lowered it, my brain ready to pack the shipment away and head back to the temple, but my body froze.

"Hi."

She was beautiful. A siren right out of the sailor stories my father used to tell me. Her lips were soft and pink, smooth. Eyes the colour of dawn over the river, hair like fire. She smiled at me over the box.

"I'm Morgann. What's your name, Apprentice?"

Warmth flushed through my body and my breath stuttered. An uncertain whine was the only sound I could make. I was dimly aware of the box lid shutting in front of me. My eyes wanted to cling to her face, and yet they couldn't resist traveling downwards, taking in the vest that shaped subtle curves over the loose shirt and pants she wore, thin fabric clinging to the top of her hips as she moved—

Oh, blessed spirits, she was walking around the table towards me.

"H-ha-uh. Hada." I swallowed, face burning as she stopped in front of me. I had enough of my mother in me that it wouldn't show, but I could feel it. Thankful for the first time in my life for my loose black robes, I tucked my hands inside the sleeves. Just because an unfairly attractive girl was looking at me like *that* wasn't any reason for me to get flustered.

"Hada," she said, rolling the sound, tasting my name on her tongue. Voice somehow earthy and breathy all at once. I couldn't help it—I wanted her to taste other parts of me that way. She reached up a hand, "You have beautiful hair, Hada."

Dark as the robes I wore, soft waves framed my face, short below my ears and even shorter in the back. Most people mistook me for a boy, especially with a Yalloran name—

"I've never seen another girl with hair like yours."

Oh, by the burnt bones in my ancestors' graves. Her fingers felt like silk against my skin as they brushed my cheek. She was so close I could see a faint smudge of dirt on her shirt collar. I mumbled something incoherent; I don't even know what I was trying to say.

She stepped back, head tilted to one side, a small smile playing around her lips.

"It was nice to meet you, Hada." I swear she winked at me, hips swaying as she walked away while I stood there, jaw open like a stunned camel.

Time passed, I'm not sure how much. The merchant came out. I was still staring off into the growing crowds of people. He nudged me, a raised eyebrow indicating that I should be off before I scared away his customers.

Normally I would have cringed but . . . all I could think of was her. Grabbing the box, I hurried off to the temple. I *had* to tell Glyn about this.

❧

Late, as usual, I dashed through the temple gates, weaving around other apprentices doing chores in the courtyard. Taking the main steps two at a time, cringing as my feet squeaked on the dark stone just inside the door way. Dust does that on these stones; smooth and black they'd been shipped from Rigaul, Necromancers unwilling to use Yalloran stone for the temple.

I peeled off to the left instead of heading into the main temple area, bowing as well as I could with my hands full of the box when I passed one of the Spirit Masters. Weaving through corridors I breathed a sigh of relief when I saw Glyn waiting for me outside of the stone room.

Glyn sort of . . . attached herself to me when I first arrived at the temple. She's like a lone clam clinging to a dock—I wonder why she's there sometimes, but I don't particularly want her to leave, either. I'm the first mixed-blood apprentice ever and not everyone's okay with that, despite the accord the Yallora and the Rigaullans reached years ago.

But Glyn doesn't care, and she knows I hate being alone in the stone room, so she waits for me, even though she's on library duty instead.

"You're late."

I rolled my eyes. Glyn has the angular bones of the Rigaullans instead of my rounder, wider Yalloran features. Unfairly tall, she's lean and brown all over from our sun and she towers over me. Sometimes—like right now—she'll try to use that to intimidate me. It doesn't work.

Well . . . maybe a little.

"There was a girl at the merchant's tent," I said, pushing through the carved doors of the stone room.

"Oh, really?" Glyn followed behind me, hanging back as I set my box on the table in the middle of the room.

The stone room was carved from one massive block of black stone several shades darker than my skin, floated across the ocean and transported here through Rigaullan magic. It's the very foundation of the temple. Niches are carved into the walls themselves, holding every type of stone imaginable. Even the table—inset with spells and inscriptions for purifying, stabilizing, and sorting stones—is part of the original block.

There are no windows. Crystal globes set into the walls give off light; I love and hate this room. I can hear the stones sing—pure, resonating joy and undiluted earth-power—but they also sing the shrieks of my ancestors; they remember the feel and smell and blood of the Yallora burnt alive when the Rigaullan ships first landed, greasy smoke still embedded deep in some of the stones.

Contrary to common belief, a Necromancer's magic starts inside. We can't heal the souls of others—mending rifts in hearts and minds, banishing nightmares, easing fear, sorrow, grief—if we're not whole and balanced ourselves.

I touched one of the purification stones on the edge of the table and breathed out the memories. Not everyone has to do this; not everyone can hear the stones. It's why they took me—it's a rare gift, one that's supposed to make learning easier but has done the opposite for me. It's too rare for the temple to pass up, regardless of what's in my blood.

"So what's so special about this girl?" Glyn leaned on the table when I was done. She might not understand what this room does to me, but she respects how I feel about it.

Avoiding her gaze, I brushed specks of red sand off the box.

"She was just really, really pretty."

"So?"

"And she said hi to me." I traced a spiralling glyph on the lid, sure that if I was just a few shades paler my face would be glowing red.

"She said hi, to you? Really? That's a good sign, right?" Frowning a little, Glyn crossed her arms.

I rolled my eyes. "Yes, it's a good sign. People generally say hi to one another when they're interested in another person."

She gave me a look—half smile, half exasperation, somehow both annoyed and bemused.

"I wouldn't know about that now, would I?"

I gave her a look. That look. The "stop shitting around and help me" look. She looked back. The "but why, it's so much fun" look. We had a little staring contest, bugging our eyes out at one another before dissolving into giggles.

"Okay, fine, you win." Glyn brushed a strand of her hair out of her face. "So why don't you track this girl down and get to know her better?"

I shrugged, fiddling with the lock.

"Can't. Apprentice, remember? Want to, but can't."

"Sure you can. I mean, I'm not inclined that way, but we don't take the chastity vows until we get our moonstones. You can sleep with whoever you want before that. And if it gets really serious you can just not get the final chip." She wiggled the ring on her right hand.

Her spectrolite chip glimmered in the crystal-diffused light, chalcedony and jet shimmering softly. The rings track our progress, different stones set in a band of silver and jet showing our progression towards mastery. Mine only has a pale green spot of chalcedony.

I sighed. "Yeah, but I'm already a chip behind you and everyone else. You know most of the teachers don't want me here. I can't afford to get caught doing anything. If I get thrown out . . . " My voice faded out. Glyn new as well as I did that my father would starve if I didn't send him most of the allowance the temple gave me.

She gave my arm a comforting squeeze. "I know. Your dad."

I nodded before opening the lid. "And besides I—oh, blessed burning spirits."

"What?" Glyn straightened as I froze, one hand holding up the box lid. I kept staring at the empty spot inside of it.

"There's two bags." I whirled to face Glyn. "There's only two bags. How can there be two? There were three. Three, one for each day in the cycle—soul, body, mind, three facets, three ceremonies, three deliveries to pick up before the rotation changes, three—"

"Hada! You're babbling." Glyn's hands were on my shoulders, pressing down to still tremors I hadn't noticed.

"I know, but there should be three!" Pulling away from her, I started to pace, chewing at the side of my thumb. My teeth worrying at the callous there from years of making fishnets with my father.

"Did you check before you left?"

"Of course I checked! No one came near the box except—" I stopped talking. Oh, shit.

"Um, Hada—" Glyn gently lay a hand on my arm "—I think that girl might have been interested in more than just you."

❧

You'd think a merchant who served the three temples would be a lot more helpful. Instead, he brushed me off. Said he'd never seen Morgann and that I had, in fact, received the delivery, complete. Losing it was my problem.

I wanted to punch him.

Instead I wandered into the midday crowds, sweltering in my robes and a little lost as to how to track down a thief hiding a shipment of water stones. Time was slipping away; we needed the stones for tonight's ritual, and while Glyn and I had unpacked, purified, and stored what remained of the shipment, my mistake would be discovered by sundown, ending my future with the temple, and any hope I had of keeping my father alive.

Sure, we have enough water stones to get through the next few days, but the Yallora shamans can only stabilize them for so long. After that, they dissolve, so we can never have more than a day or two's stones in reserve. I had lost a whole day's worth of water stones; expulsion would be *kind.*

And water stones go fast. Rigaullan black markets pay a lot for them—for healing, desert journeys, backdoor magic workings not supported by the temples. Even if I found my thief, she might not have the stones any more, I thought, staring at the water fountain in front of the Healer's temple. Several Healer apprentices nodded at me as they moved past, marker bracelets flashing on their wrists, similar to my ring.

I pretended to not see them. I don't like the Healers much. Most of them refuse to accept that anything in the desert can heal; they frown on Yallora medicines and remedies like the ones that my mother used to keep my father alive. Instead they import expensive Rigaulan herbs, growing what they can, irrigating when they have to. It's a waste of knowledge and (a much bigger crime) a waste of water. But they treat Necromancers and their families for free, whereas me . . .

Well, apparently I just give away water stones to pretty girls for nothing.

Except . . . not nothing. I had her name. It could be fake, but . . .

I turned south, towards the docks. It was worth a shot.

❧

The weird looks I got this morning in the market were nothing compared to what I got as I picked my way around piles of garbage littering the south-side alleys. Littered with alcoves, spaces in the brick look out on the water. Dead ends without docks, abandoned over the years. No one uses them so the poor camp here, fishing what they can with makeshift nets, scraping clams off the pier.

It's dirty and unwashed and it smells like dirt and fish and salt. It smells like home. It is home.

I grew up here, under the feet of sailors and fishmongers, watching them come and go. Sitting for hours listening to their stories, the gossip and rumours, their fantastic tales of life at sea and faraway places. Princes and gods and bewitching sirens and women so beautiful it hurts to look at them.

I have no desire to see those places—this land is my home. Though he'll never return to it, the sea calls to my father's blood, not mine. It's something he shares with the other beggars. That's why I'm here. The poor near the water have their own community; they hear things, know things. Can sometimes feel them in the air.

My skin itched, remembering the feel of clothes I hadn't worn in six years. Sandstone walls singing to me of the child I used to be. I gathered my robes to stop them dragging on the ground; there would be questions asked I didn't want to answer if I came home covered in alley gunk.

As I inched down the alley a misshapen lump at the end turned out to be a man; old and bent, scraggly beard greying in patches. Sitting in a little nest of rags with more clinging to his thin shoulders. He didn't move as I came closer.

Everyone calls him Dockson. No one knows where he came from, he's just always been here, on the docks, and no one knows his real name. I'm not sure if he even remembers it after all this time. My father once told me Dockson had been Dockson for longer than he'd been alive.

I sat down beside him waves and sea bird cries filling the space between us. It was a larger gap than it had ever been, but not, I thought, uncrossable.

"How is he?" I asked, after a time, picking up a net to mend.

"The money you send—that helps." His eyes weren't remarkable—but the way he looked at me, the pull of the skin around his eyelids, it was like he'd stabbed those ragged fingernails right into my chest.

"But he'd be better if you were still here."

I shook my head. My ring—though mostly air—was heavy on my finger.

"They're not so bad. At the temple. He has enough to eat, right?" My eyes followed my hands as I helped weave the net back together. Before I'd left, I'd been able to do this in my sleep.

Dockson sighed. "More than. And a strong roof over his head now. But he misses you."

"I miss him, too."

"What did you come here for, Hada?"

Grabbing his gaze, holding it, I silently begged him to help me. "I need information. I lost a shipment of water stones and if I don't get them back by sunset I'll probably be expelled."

Dockson said nothing.

"You know he can't work with his leg, Dockson. And the two of us couldn't mend enough nets to keep one of us fed, let alone both. Please. The temple is my only chance to help. If I get expelled—"

Dockson held up a hand to stop me. Words dried on my lips, blowing away on the salty air. I didn't have to say that nowhere else would take me, that I'd never be able to get a job and I'd have to go back to scrounging for scraps on the street. Dockson was there with us. He knew.

"All right. What do you need?"

👄

Trust Dockson to know everything.

Well, not *everything* . . . but he did know who would know and a small silver coin was enough to get them to tell me where to find my thief.

It was midafternoon by the time I reached Morgann's house—if it could be called that. Really it was a room in an old, rotting boardinghouse in the slums, around a corner and down the far end of an alley. There was a dizzying feeling of familiarity as I walked towards it, though that could be the heat. My robes were designed to keep the sun off pale Rigaullan skin; the Yallora wear much less, more concerned with the heat, dark skin protection enough from the sun.

Nausea roiled in my stomach, cramping and queasy as I climbed the outdoor stairs to the second floor. What if she wasn't home? What if she'd already sold the stones? What if she pulled out a knife and tried to stab me?

What if I just couldn't say no to her? Given my reaction this morning, that should probably be my biggest concern.

Well, I'd just have to. A deep breath in, and I knocked on the door. When no one answered I knocked again. And again. I'd raised my fist to pound on the door when it was yanked open.

"What?"

He was Morgann's height and he looked exactly like Morgann—but he was a boy. I blinked twice. Yep, definitely a boy.

I straightened my shoulders. "Where's Morgann?"

He leaned against the doorway, arms crossed. One of his eyebrows twitched up ever so slightly. "What do you want with her, Apprentice?"

I'd swear a blood oath to the Spirit Masters at the temple that he was wearing the same clothes Morgann had been earlier. Minus the vest—the vest that she looked so good in. Wrenching my mind from that train of thought, I wedged my foot against the doorframe so he couldn't close it on me.

"That's between us now, isn't it?"

"It's really not," he said as I shoved past him. The room was small; all of these boarding houses were cramped and tiny. People packed in like dead fish at market. There was a single small window, an old scarred table that was missing chunks of wood, and a door that led somewhere—to an even smaller room, probably.

"Where is she?" I repeated.

"What do you want with her, Hada?" he asked me again and I froze. I hadn't given him my name.

He shut the door, dread creeping through me like an octopus's tentacles in my stomach. Twisting and slippery.

"How do you know my name?"

"I— Uh . . . Morgann—" he stammered, flushing and looking away.

I stepped closer, looking at his face. It wasn't *like* Morgann's face—it was her face. Hair pulled back, posture and voice changed, but it was her. Down to the speck of dirt on the shirt's collar. I was sure of it.

"Oh, burning spirits. You're Morgann."

"Right now, it's *Morgan.*" His—her?—eyes were hard, flashing. Voice deeper than Morgann's breathier tones, his words had an undercurrent of steel.

"How—"

"I'm both." He cut me off before I could finish.

"You're what?"

"I'm both. I'm Morgan and Morgann. I'm a man and a woman."

I stared at him. It was like he was talking gibberish, except . . . that look on his face. Hesitation, defiance, fear, the anticipation of violence or—even worse—invalidation. As if he expected me to deny him who he was. And underneath it all, a rock solid certainty in himself. In his own identity. It was the same look I'd had when I'd had to tell the temple mages I liked girls, or like Glyn when she'd told me she didn't like *anyone* that way.

Okay, so he was both. I didn't know how it was possible, but I believed him.

"Whatever you are, that doesn't matter." I waved my hands as if to brush it all aside. *"You stole my water stones!"*

Morgan was so surprised he looked like I'd slapped him in the face with a dead fish. It probably wasn't everyday he told people that (I don't tell people about my preferences often either) and having someone just disregard it . . . Yes, I could see why he was shocked.

My mouth was open to start yelling at him again when a cough echoed from the other room. A dry hacking wheeze, lungs not able to function.

"Morgann?" a voice croaked from the back.

He darted around me, over to the door, pulling out his hair as he went, stride and set of his shoulders changing as he moved .

His voice changed too, that breathy, earthier sound I'd heard this morning. "I'm here, Ma."

I followed him (her?) through the door.

A woman lay on a pallet on the floor, a thin, stained sheet covering most of her lower body as she shook with coughs. Morgan (Morgann?) went to her, arms wrapping around her mother. Two fiery redheads bowed together. Rubbing small circles on her back, Morgann tried to soothe the cough that wrenched the woman's body in every direction. Fluid rattled deep in her chest. Her limbs were shaking and spotted, eyes glassy with fever.

And the look on Morgann's face as I stood in that doorway—the desperation, the need, the love.

The memories came unbidden: nights of listening to my father, sweating and whimpering after he'd lost his leg. Sitting and holding his hand because it was the only thing I could do as he relived the storm every night. Loose rigging tearing his leg off again and again in his dreams. Tears leaking from the corners of his eyes because of the itch he couldn't scratch—the one that simply wouldn't go away. Ghost pains from a dead limb that wouldn't die.

I turned away, giving them their privacy.

Standing by the one small, shuttered window, I peeked through the cracks in the slats, pretending I could see outside. Pretending there was something *to* see.

Footsteps sounded behind me a while later and I turned to find myself facing Morgan as he pulled his hair back again. His shoulders were straighter, stride different. It was amazing how fast he changed.

"Sorry. I normally don't switch so fast, but . . . " A sigh, sad and resigned. "Ma doesn't want to see me. She needs Morgann. Right now, she needs her. And if you take those water stones away I can't give her much else." Even his voice was lower again, like he'd practiced this a lot.

Chewing my lip, I nodded.

Could I do that? Those water stones would buy a healer to fix any ailment his mother had ever had. But I needed them back. My father and I depended on them.

I spun the almost-empty ring on my finger.

If I let him keep the stones, both my father and I would probably starve. If I took them, his mother would die. Probably within the week.

"I need those stones back." I watched the light play across the chalcedony and jet on my ring as I spoke. My eyes couldn't meet his.

Morgan's fists clenched.

"Gods damn it, don't you have a heart? She's going to *die* if I don't—"

"You think you're the only one with someone depending on you? This isn't a game to me, Morgan. It's not a matter of having a heart, it's my father's *life.*" Shouting wasn't going to solve anything, but that didn't stop me from doing it.

He crumpled under my words, like he just couldn't stand against the world anymore. He turned away, flinching and afraid. My heart ached. He probably believed the stories about us, thought I'd curse him or take the stones by force or magic if I had to. My stomach clenched and unclenched; underneath everything else I was suddenly glad I'd missed lunch.

"They're under there." He gestured to one of the floorboards. "I had a buyer coming for them tonight. I was gonna be able to fix everything."

I could see the despair simmering in his eyes, and I knew it would eventually turn to hatred as I pried up the board and retrieved my stones, glyphs still pulsing faintly. I sat there on my knees, on the floor of a run-down room in a rotting boardinghouse, weighing the bag of stones against my conscience.

Suede tickled my fingers. Round edges dug into my palm through the bag. Hefting it, my ring caught the light.

Sighing, I tucked the bag inside my robes and pulled off my ring. Rising, I held it out to him. "Here."

Morgan frowned at me. "What . . . ?"

"Take it. Show it to any acolyte at the Healer's temple. They'll treat your mother."

He blinked before slowly inching his hand out and taking my ring. He held it like it was spun from sand, ready to wash away in the tide.

I couldn't bear the aching mix of emotions on his face—hope, joy, trepidation, relief. Because I would swear he was blinking back tears, I turned to leave.

"She doesn't know," he said. I stopped in the doorframe, not sure if he was talking about himself or stealing the stones.

"She doesn't know and she doesn't *need* to know. She's got enough to worry about. She wouldn't understand anyway." His head drooped in defeat, voice sad and just a little bitter.

Both, definitely both, but more about him than the theft, I thought, crossing over to him.

"Hey—" I laid a hand on his slumped shoulder, pushing him back so he looked at me. "You'd be surprised what parents will understand."

I smiled at him and he smiled back, his hand coming up to cover mine.

"How'd you end up with them anyway?" he asked, head tilted ever so slightly.

I shrugged. "I was about ten when I got scouted at one of the annual sweeps. Had power, talent. Lots of it they said. Da tried to stop me, but I went anyway. They train the magic into ya, the streets out of ya, but I haven't forgotten. I still send him money so he has enough to eat."

"That sounds terrible."

"It's not that bad. This way I know he's alive, even if he won't see me."

Morgan seemed to catch it—the inflection in my voice that said my father didn't care about the girls; he won't forgive me for choosing the temple over him.

"That's a shame. It's his loss." Morgan's eyes stared into mine and I started to feel a little dizzy from the warmth in his eyes. Which was weird because *that* had never happened before. Not with a boy.

But he was also sometimes a girl. A really *pretty* girl. And a just-as-handsome boy.

I pulled back, tucking my hands inside my sleeves and discreetly checking to make sure the bag of water stones was still in its place.

"So, uh, what do you . . . uh . . . " I knew I should leave—both because of the way he was looking at me and because of the slant of the afternoon shadows on the floor—but I had to ask. This boy-girl-person was confusing for me.

He shrugged. "I just like people. Parts have never been an issue."
I nodded, sort of getting it, but not really.

"And the other thing?"

"You know how you feel different and behave different when you
wear different sets of clothes?" Another nod from me. Yeah. That was
a feeling I knew well. "Sometimes I wake up and I feel like I'm a girl,
and sometimes I wake up and feel like I'm a boy. But I'm still *me*, I'm
just . . . " He trailed off, not quite able to get the words right.

"Interacting differently based on how you feel?"

"Yeah. That's it." He smiled at me again.

The afternoon sun filtered in at weird angles through the window
slats and lit up his cheekbones. With his hair pulled back like that,
he looked even better than he had this morning. A fluttery, sinking
feeling started up in my stomach.

Shit. Shit and fish dung and the blood on my ancestors' graves.
This was not good.

I needed to get out of there.

"Thank you." I paused in the doorway again. When I turned back
he was watching me. "The Healer's temple is open until sundown.
If you hurry you can get your mother there before the gates close."

I fled before I could see him smile again.

❧

I ran all the way back to the temple, skidding through the gates about
a half hour before sundown. Lateness is a habit of mine, so nobody
questioned it when they saw me running through the corridors.

Exhausted, it took every ounce of willpower I had left to par-
ticipate in the sundown ritual. I spent the entire ceremony trying
to catch Glyn's eye, attempting to tell her, without words, that she
should walk with me when the ceremony was over.

Her room was closer (and more private than mine as it's at the end
of a hall, not in the middle) and as soon as the door shut I flopped
on her bed, groaning in relief.

Glyn sat in the reading chair by the window, moonlight a puddle
around her.

"Since you're not dead, you got them back, right?"

Glyn's pillow was soft as I moved my face up and down, trying to nod into the feathers.

"And?"

"And what?" She probably couldn't hear me too well as I was speaking inside the pillow.

"What happened with Morgann?"

I rolled over, telling my story to the ceiling in as few words as I could. Glyn sat rapt the whole time, chin propped on her hand, nose wrinkling as I described the docks and slums to her.

"So what are you going to do now?" Glyn folded her legs beneath her on the chair, looking pensive.

"Do? Glyn, I'm going to forget any of this ever happened." It was a feeble protest—she'd pried my reaction to Morgan out of me and my cheeks felt hot.

"Three silver coins says you're not going to be able to forget her. Him? Her? Did you ask how Morgan—er—Morgann wanted to be addressed?"

I rolled my eyes. "No. I should have thought of that. He—er, she? Probably thinks I'm super inconsiderate now," I mumbled the last bit to myself. Glyn didn't need to hear me beat myself up.

"I highly doubt that."

Of course she'd heard. I stuck out my tongue at her.

"What? I might not do sexual or romantic relationships, Hada, but it sounds to me like—" She tripped over the name again.

"He was Morgan when I left, so call him Morgan."

"It sounds to me like Morgan is interested in . . . getting to know you." She said it in the dirtiest way possible. I thought about throwing the pillow at her but didn't. My arms were too tired and it felt too nice beneath my head.

"Spirits to Glyn—I like girls. And he's—"

"A girl. Sometimes."

I gave her a glare to make spirits quake. She blinked back at me like a particularly insolent catfish.

"Besides, chastity vows!" I reminded her. "It's not like I can do anything about it anyway. No matter how . . . confusing this . . . thing might be. Not happening."

Glyn studied her nails. "You've got at least six years before you earn your moonstone. You've got time to figure it out. Besides, you know it wouldn't be confusing if you weren't considering it."

I groaned, burying my face in her pillow. The absolute *worst* part about being friends with Glyn is that she's often right.

The Heart of Spring
Maria Dones

Yuki could read what was in humans' hearts. It was the reason she was able to freeze them. Yuki would linger over her victim as he slept, watching his chest rise and fall. Pressing one hand on his chest and the other on his face, she would close her eyes and feel the warmth of his heart: the soft beats of his memories, dreams and desires. With long hair swaying on either side of her face, she would purse her lips and whistle a swirling, misty breath that would ensure the icy slumber of the one who lay before her.

But as Yuki studied the teenage boy she was hunched over, she faltered. She'd found him sleeping outside the front door of a palace, the large estate of a *daimyo* lord with sloping roofs and gardens of snow. The ink black of his hair had caught her interest in the world of white this country had become. In all her years, she'd never seen a human sleeping outside in this weather.

The boy was beautiful, but all of Yuki's victims were. His top knot was falling apart in loose strands that whipped across his face, and his skin was almost as pale as Yuki's. His blue lips matched her own. But he wasn't like her—he was sleeping as all the others had been. Sleep was a stranger to Yuki.

She saw a twitch out of the corner of her eye and looked down to see his left hand trembling from the cold. But where was his other hand? Her silver eyes trailed from his face to his other arm which was extended upward. A thick rope snaked around his wrist, binding him to the brass door handle. How strange. Was this boy an enemy of the noble who lived here? But it was no matter. His heart would be frozen just as all the others. She put a hand to his face and one to his chest. But something was wrong. There was no warmth in this heart.

"Wh-who are you?"

Yuki looked up to see two eyes narrowed at her. The warm brown was striking against the pale skin and harshness of his cheekbones.

"I came here to freeze your heart," she said.

The boy sat up, his kimono rustling around him. His eyes widened in fear, but then he looked down at his feet.

"About time. I've been here every night for the last week." His tone was casual, but Yuki could see his free hand was shaking as it ran through his hair. His gaze trailed to the side. "I wonder if he'll be happy I'm gone. Or sad that he won't be able to tie me out here any longer."

"Well, whoever 'he' is, I suppose you'll never know. I can't freeze a heart that's already frozen."

"What does that mean?"

"That's my specialty. That's how I take lives and live on—feeding on the warmth of human hearts. I could still freeze the rest of you, but what would taking your life accomplish?" She glanced down at him. "Besides, you're the first one I've met who has a heart so cold. Fascinating, but of no use to me."

He sighed and blew a strand of hair away from his face. His words trembled as they came out. "Typical. Not even Death will help me."

She smiled, the tug at her lips feeling unfamiliar. "I am not Death."

"A spirit, then?"

"I won't say anything else. No one's supposed to know about me." She looked around. There was no noise coming from inside or candles flickering from the windows. Everyone else must have been asleep. "What about you? Why were you left out here?"

"I can't say. No one's supposed to know about me."

She raised her eyebrow. Were all humans like this? She'd never actually spoken to one. "Are you teasing me, human?"

"That depends. Would you kill me if I said yes?"

"I could. If I felt there was a need to."

"Aren't demons supposed to be ruthless?"

"Demon? I thought you believed me a spirit?"

"Well, your beauty had me fooled at first. And I'd never pictured a demon to look the same age as me. But you did come here to freeze my heart after all."

She laughed, a warm sound that felt strange rumbling in her throat. "You flatter me, human. But no matter, I must go find someone else's heart to freeze. Don't tell anyone about me for I will know, and I won't spare you the next time."

And with a swirl of mist and ice, she faded into the snow blowing around her.

❧

For the next few days, Yuki watched over the palace. She made sure to pass by once a day and convinced herself the fixation she had on the boy was due to his strange heart. Usually, Yuki would pass by as a gust of wind and snow. Sometimes she would allow her body to materialize and press her hands on the windows, leaving frost prints on the rice paper. One day, the boy looked back in time to see her shadow. She felt her cheeks warm and quickly faded away into wind and snow. Yuki had never blushed before, and it felt like fire on her cheek.

The boy brought the lord his meals and tended to chores around the palace. It was almost shameful to see a boy who was almost a man in such a low position. But then again, the looks of disdain the lord gave him were suspicious. And every night, his wrist was chained to the door.

"Why does the lord punish you like this?" she asked him one night, when her curiosity got the best of her. She'd caught him right as he'd been about to fall asleep in front of the door. He sat up in shock as she appeared in front of him.

"Wh-what?"

"The noble who lives here. Why he does he lock you outside? He doesn't treat any of the other servants like this."

"You think I'm a servant? I don't even know why I'm surprised."

"Just answer my question. Snow demons aren't the most patient of creatures."

"Snow demons? There's more than one?"

"Oh, well, I assume so. There must be, because there are barriers I can't pass in this land. That must be their territory."

"You mean, you've never met another?"

"Never."

"Then how do you know snow demons aren't patient? Maybe other snow demons could wait a lifetime to hear why I'm always tied out here."

"Or maybe other snow demons would have killed you on sight."

He smiled wearily, looking her up and down as he seemed to realize once again what she was. "If there are no others, how did you know what you had to do when you were born? Or rather, created?"

"I've known since the beginning who I am and what my duty is to winter."

"Doesn't it get lonely?"

Yuki was starting to feel uncomfortable. There was so much she didn't know about who she was and how she came to be. Having someone else know made her feel vulnerable. Weak. And she was starting to feel a tightening in her chest. When she looked down, she saw that her hands had gained some colour—a soft pink in her fingertips that had never been in there. Yuki wasn't sure what would happen if she kept speaking to him, but maybe it wasn't worth the risk. She opened her mouth to speak.

"I'm a demon. I don't feel things the same way you do."

"But—"

"I've had enough. I don't know why I talked to you in the first place. Humans aren't supposed to know how or why I do things."

"Wait—"

But before the boy could finish, Yuki was gone.

❧

For the next week, Yuki avoided the palace altogether. Instead, she focused all of her energy from human hearts to making the winds howl and the snow fall in icy rocks. People stayed indoors, and sometimes when she spied, she caught whispers of children frightened that winter would last forever.

Occasionally, when her thoughts drifted to the boy, she felt herself go weak. It became hard to summon snow and cold. To remedy this, she would sneak in through the cracks of doors and windows and freeze someone's life away. But something was wrong. She felt herself hesitating before stealing the warmth from a victim, a hesitation that frightened her. Killing had never been hard before. Yuki was nature's way of commanding death in order to keep the world balanced. There was no reason for her to feel guilt, but she couldn't deny that it had been a lot easier to kill humans before she'd met one.

One night, Yuki convinced herself to go see the boy. After all, she had been acting like she was scared of him. It was laughable to think of herself as scared of a human. She passed by the palace just as day was turning into night. But when she went to the door, there was no boy. Yuki passed by the windows, drifting to every part of the estate. There were servants and women, but no sign of the boy. Then, just as she was about to give up, she heard a scream coming from the front door.

"Worthless . . . good-for-nothing . . . spoiled . . . " the noble muttered. He kicked the screaming boy just as Yuki got to the front door. He was wearing a kimono and armour—the signature look of a wealthy landowner. Yuki didn't materialize in front of him, but he must have felt her presence because he laughed and said, "I hope you enjoy your rest tonight. It seems like it'll be the coldest night of the year. Let's see if you can survive this time."

The noble tied the boy's wrist to the handle, went inside, and closed the door behind him hard enough to make it hurt. The boy's back slammed against the door. He whimpered but stopped when Yuki appeared in front of him. He smiled—a strange smile with tense lips and bitter eyes.

"Why are you here? Did you decide to kill me after all?" He

motioned to the bruises all over his body. "Go ahead. Half the job has already been done for you."

"You never answered my question."

"What question?"

"Why are you kept out here? Why does he punish you like this?" He patted the ground next to him. "Tell you what. I'll tell you about me if you sit here next to me and tell me about yourself."

"You know there are things I cannot tell you."

"I know. I'll stop asking if it makes you uncomfortable."

Yuki hesitated for a moment but then sat next to him. Why not humour him? Besides, she wasn't sure why, but she wanted to know more about this boy and why his heart was so cold. Was he a bad person? Did he deserve the punishments he was receiving? It was silent between them for a moment, and then the boy spoke.

"I'm not a servant."

Yuki looked over at him. "What?"

"Well, I'm not technically a servant. I'm his son. The noble's, I mean."

"But if you're his son, why does he keep you out here?"

"His wife died. My mother. Giving birth to me." He turned to her and forced a laugh. "You know what's funny?"

Yuki was silent.

"When I was younger, I used to think I was some sort of demon, the way he talked about my birth. Like I had ripped my way out of her stomach with my claws and cried on her corpse as she lay there in a bed of blood."

Yuki didn't know how to respond. So she changed the subject instead. "But that doesn't explain why he keeps you out here. Love or no love, aren't sons highly-prized by nobles?"

The boy nodded. "He tried to love me at first. But I think all he saw in me was his face with the eyes and lips of a woman he could no longer have." The boy smirked, his lip bleeding slightly from earlier. "Or maybe all he saw was the face of her murderer."

Yuki put a finger to his lips. For a moment, their eyes both lingered on the red on her finger. She quickly wiped it on the ground next to her and looked away from him. "Sorry. It was distracting."

"My lips were distracting to you?" he asked, raising his eyebrow.

She laughed but tried to cover it up with her hand. "Not in the way you're suggesting."

He looked at her, offended. "Why are you laughing? I may look beat up right now, but I'll have you know, I look nice when I'm not tied to the door of a building."

Yuki smiled. "I'll take your word for it, mortal." It was silent between them for a few moments—Yuki could hear his breathing getting heavier and the wind rustling through his shaggy hair. She opened her mouth to speak. "Now, back to your explanation. When did he start punishing you?"

"He's always slapped me around, but that's not uncommon for noble fathers. Apparently, a couple of weeks ago, one of his friends came over and was astonished that my father had only one son."

"Is that uncommon?" Yuki asked, wrapping her arms around her knees.

He nodded. "Most nobles have many wives and even more children. His friend told him to keep me protected since apparently heirs are often kidnapped from wealthy men for ransom. Ever since then, he had the idea of tying me out here. As if to say, 'Take him if you want him!'" He snorted. "It always makes him laugh, to tie me out here. The ultimate dishonour. At first he was baffled that I didn't die out here, but now I think he enjoys it so he can do it all over again."

She didn't know what to say. He looked so defeated, shivering in the cold. But the cold would not take the life of someone like him. "It's no wonder your heart is already frozen."

"What makes you say that?"

"You have no one to love you or look after you. Humans seem to need that to be happy."

"And snow demons?"

She shook her head. "Snow demons cannot love."

"How do you know if you've never met one before?"

"I—I don't know." She looked out at the snowy landscape. I should go."

And she turned back into wind and snow as he watched. But, instead of leaving, she made a wind barrier around him so the cold wouldn't reach him. He stopped shivering and smiled.

"Nice try. But I know you're still there."

❦

For the next week she looked over the palace, but never appeared before the boy. Sometimes, when she became a barrier around his shivering form, he would beg her to materialize, but she refused. He finally convinced her when he shouted up at her one night.

"You promised! You promised you would tell me about you. I told you about me." She sighed as she materialized next to him. He was startled at the sight of her. "I—I didn't think that would actually work."

"Let's just say you wore me down."

"About time."

"So what did you want to ask me?" she asked, annoyed at the silly grin on his face.

"Are you as cold as you look?"

"What?"

He grabbed her hand and squeezed it. The heat from his hand sent goosebumps up her spine. "It's like touching ice. Do you know what it's like to be warm?"

She yanked her hand away. It was unnerving, how unafraid he was of her. "I can feel the warmth of others as I freeze their heart. And I could feel your warmth when you touched me. But no one's ever done that before."

"Guess that makes me lucky."

She snorted. "Lucky? You're tied to a door."

"Yeah, but you see, you were wrong before. I do have someone who looks after me now. A girl."

"Oh." Yuki wasn't sure why, but suddenly the warmth in her hands—that she hadn't noticed until now—left her hands as quickly as it had come.

He smiled at the look on her face. "I'm talking about you."

"Me?" she asked, pointing to herself.

He laughed. "I've seen you peek at me through the windows in the house. You're not as good at blending in as you think you are."

She felt the heat return to her hands and spread to her cheeks. "I just . . . You're . . . "

"I'm what?"

"Fascinating."

"Fascinating?"

"Because of your heart."

"Oh. Right."

She looked down at her hands. There was colour in them again. She was no longer as pale as the snow. Yuki looked almost . . . human. Her chest tightened with fear. What was talking to this boy doing to her? What was it doing to him? She swallowed and scooted close to him before putting her head on his chest. And it was just as she'd thought

"Your heart . . . it's no longer frozen." And then it all became clear when she felt his heart speed up as she pressed her cheek against his kimono. "Y-you love me," she said, her eyes wide with shock. "But you can't. I shouldn't even be here. I'm not supposed to talk to humans."

"But—"

"I'm sorry. But we can't do this anymore." Yuki put her hand on the rope connecting him to the door. The rope turned to ice, which she broke in half. She wasn't supposed to interfere with human affairs like this—but she had to make sure he'd be all right.

"Please don't go," he begged, grabbing her wrist.

"I have to. But I'll make sure the cold won't harm you. Please, run away. Find a new life for yourself. The cold won't harm you even without your frozen heart." She kissed him on the cheek, an icy tear trailing down her cheek. "You have my protection."

And as quickly as she had appeared, she disappeared.

●

For the next month, she stayed far away from the palace, not wanting to be reminded of him. The way the cold left her when she was with him scared her. One day, as she was about to freeze the heart of a sleeping farmer, she felt an unsettling chill down her spine. In her head she heard words that were not her own. *"You'll see! The girl made of snow will come for me! And I'll make sure she kills me this time!"*

It was him. He'd told someone about her. And now, he would pay the price. Killing was simple. It was something she always did, something she had to do. It was how she lived, how she kept winter strong. So why did she feel dread at the prospect of freezing the life out of someone who was practically a stranger? But this boy wasn't exactly a stranger. Not to someone like her. Not to someone who had never spoken to another.

"Why did you do it?" she asked him, when she finally materialized at the palace. It was nighttime, and once again, his hand was tied to the doorknob, and he was sprawled out in front of the door.

"Because I wanted to see you."

Yuki grabbed him by the collar of his kimono. "Very funny. Now tell me the truth."

He winced at the newfound tension in his arm from being pulled towards her and the door. "Koichi," he whispered, coughing slightly. "That's my name. You should know it before you kill me."

She bit her lip and gazed at him. Something was off. "You want to die, don't you? You spoke of me knowing fully well what I would do."

"There's nothing left for me. Not anymore."

"Why didn't you run away from this place? I gave you my protection."

"What's the point? You didn't find me worthwhile enough to keep around. No one does."

Yuki narrowed her eyes at him. "It's not that I didn't find you worthwhile. I was trying to protect both of us. Talking to you makes me weak. I'm pretty sure I would have disappeared if we had kept talking."

"Then—then you do love me."

She shook her head. "It doesn't matter. You need to find a human to love. Someone who can stay with you and love the same way you can."

"What if you make me like you?"

She kneeled next to him, putting her hand on his shoulder and trying not to quiver. "That's not possible. And even if it was, snow demons can't be with another. I've known this since I was created. We need to keep our own hearts cold to keep winter alive."

"But it isn't."

"Excuse me?"

"Your hand feels warm on my shoulder," Koichi said, a grin on his face.

She looked down and sighed. Her hand had regained a flush of pink. Soon, the warmth would spread to the rest of her body. There was no point in trying to stop it anymore. This boy would be her destruction. She sat next to him and put her head on his shoulder. He rested his own head on hers as her eyes closed.

"Don't you have to kill me or something?"

"I wouldn't give you the satisfaction."

He laughed, and for the first time, Yuki fell into sleep like it was something she had always been able to do.

☙

The next morning, the noble of the palace walked outside to see Koichi lying on the ground. Surrounding the boy was a halo of snowflakes, which didn't seem to want to melt. When the noble tried to shake his son awake, he realized the boy had no more breaths left in him. He looked out into the distance to see that the world was no longer caught in a snowstorm. Spring was coming.

Looking Good
Deborah Walker

The first thing I noticed about the new girl was that she wasn't wearing the school colours on her face. I had never seen a pupil of McAllister Girls' Academy, a major or a minor, without the school badge on her skin. Then I noticed that her hair was kind of frizzy and that it looked real.

"She must be an anti-synth," said Alicia incredulously. "Wow. I've read about them, but I never thought I'd meet one. What a freak."

"Why would anybody be anti-synth?" asked Jeddy. "They'd have to deal with all kinds of killer diseases. I just can't imagine anybody being so dumb. It's so retro and not in a good way. She must be a freak."

I remembered that there was an anti-synth community somewhere in the Midlands, maybe in Nottingham. They were called Charlies. They lived without any synthetic gene technologies.

"It's a religious thing," I said, staring at the new girl. She looked so strange walking through the school without the school colours. She looked naked, somehow. I realized that, for the first time, I was looking at a person without any synthetic mods. She looked pretty good to me, attractive, even. I turned back to the canteen table, and I saw that Alicia and Jeddy were staring at me. Alicia and Jeddy were my best friends.

"What do you think, Marjory?" asked Alicia.

"She must be a freak," I said.

Turned out that Ella wasn't a Charlie. Mrs. McAllister, the school's headmistress, explained it all to us when she brought Ella into class. Ella was disabled. She had an anomalous genome that wouldn't allow any click DNA insertions. She had some kind of crazy, ultra-efficient immune system that just ate up any foreign DNA that tried to enter her body.

"I've got Metchnikoff Syndrome. It's my macrophage assembly. It's incredibly effective—a hint of foreign DNA and . . . zap."

Mrs. McAllister had assigned me as Ella's buddy, and I was showing her around the school. She didn't seem to mind talking about her disability. I thought that was pretty cool.

"Can't they mod your phages, and make them less effective or something?" I asked.

"Nah. As soon as they try to insert any type of foreign DNA, my macrophages leap into action. The transformation chemicals that suppress the immune system during click DNA insertions just don't seem to work for me. It's complicated, there's a whole host of other bits and bobs involved, but the macrophages are the main part of my trouble. They just cannot get any foreign DNA into me, so, therefore, no lovely clickable DNA for me."

"That's tough," I said. I couldn't imagine it.

Ella seemed to shrug it off, "Nah. It's not so bad. Mum and Dad, though, it's harder for them. They just won't accept it. I can't tell you how many medical procedures I've been through."

"Hmm," I said, putting a sympathetic hand on her arm.

"So when I turned thirteen, I just said, 'enough is enough'. No more medical procedures for me. They couldn't do anything about it, once I'd reached the age of majority."

"Hmm." I couldn't stop looking at her.

"Mum and Dad are pretty upset about it, though. They think I should keep on trying, and the government, they would just love to get their hands on my body."

I smiled. I thought about making a comment then thought better of it.

"Why don't you come over to my place tonight?" she asked.

"I'd love to."

She smiled and I just couldn't get over how I was looking at the real her. She had freckles, slightly crooked teeth, but they weren't quirks to make her look better. They weren't deliberate imperfections to set off her beauty. She was the real deal.

I told my so-called best friends that I was going to go to Ella's house, and they were a bit off about it.

"You don't waste much time, do you, Marjory?" said Alicia.

"I don't know what you mean," I said, feigning ignorance.

"I mean this is her first day at school, and you've already got a date."

"It's not a date."

"Don't you think she's a bit strange, Marjory?" asked Jeddy. "I mean Alicia's just concerned about you. Sometimes it's not such a good idea to get too friendly with the weirdos."

Jeddy was always the peacemaker. The thing was, me and Alicia had one of those "on and off" things. It was "off" at the moment and I saw no reason why they should choose my girlfriends, I mean my friends.

"I'm going over to her house, that's all. Ella could do with a friend."

Alicia and Jeddy exchanged significant glances and then turned back to the console's lesson.

❧

Ella had her own suite of rooms connected to her parents' house. It was definitely not an anti-synth residence.

"Wow," I said. A 3-D fabber took up a sizeable portion of her fabroom. I noticed that it was hooked up to a personal synth power source; the new fabbers use up an awful lot of energy. "This is a full-size, people model. Wow. They cost a bundle, what do you parents do?"

"Dad's a patent lawyer and Mum's a campaigner, but I paid for the fabber. That's why I've got my own power supply. Mum and Dad say I've got to pay my own energy bills."

"Where on earth do you get the money from?" I asked.

"Different governments and different research institutes pay a lot of money to study me. Remember my super-immune system? They think I might be the next cure for cancer."

"That's pretty awesome." Then I remembered what she had told me, about no more medical procedures. "Don't you want to help them?" I asked.

She shrugged, "They've got a copy of my genome, let them work on that for a few years. They want to study my immune system in vivo, but I said, give me a few years off, let me enjoy my majority years and just be normal, for a change."

She would never be normal, but she didn't have to be. She was just great the way she was, but I was actually more interested in trying out the fabber.

"Can we fab a copy of the CheeseDolls?" The CheeseDolls were my favourite band.

"Sure," said Ella, typing in the commands. "I love the CheeseDolls, too." She frowned when she checked the supply of memory-plastic in the hopper. "I'm afraid I'm going to have to create them half size."

Half size—it would take me six-month's allowance to afford that. "Sure," I said.

The figures of the CheeseDolls materialized in front of us, programed with a copy of their latest album. We sat back on the couch and let the plastic robots do their stuff. Their wonderful, discordant music washed over us.

◡

The first thing I did when I got back to my own suite of rooms, (how I love being majority, it's so great to have some privacy), was to switch on my clickable mirror. I set it to display an image of my current face then I played around with the click DNA inserts to see how each would fit in with my current sequences and my native DNA. Adding click DNA is a subtle process, each fragment is designed to slip into your genome. The software in the clickable mirror gives a pretty good simulation of how you're going to look.

I spent a long time at my mirror wondering what face Ella would find the most attractive. It had to be subtle. I couldn't just go into school with a new face next week and expect her to fall in love with me. I also spent a lot of time trying to fathom the various theories about attractiveness. Attractiveness is a big industry with too many contradictory theories for me to understand.

I kinda felt a bit guilty thinking about Ella. She wouldn't be able to change her face; maybe I was taking advantage. But then I thought "beauty is only gene deep," after all. I finally found a look I was happy with and downloaded the click DNA patches. I pressed them onto my face. They sank immediately into my skin and began to do their magic. Come next week, I would be what I had guessed Ella would find the most attractive. How could she resist me?

◡

It didn't quite work out like that, but over the next month, we got pretty close. We did girl stuff together, we did each other's hair, we gossiped, we listened to music together. I was waiting until the right time to make my move.

I went over to Ella's suite most nights. She had a hard time studying; she was stuck in the remedial classes. You can't just click in knowledge, but you can click in intelligence enhancers. It didn't seem fair that Ella had to study without the proper tools.

"Arrghh! I just can't get my head around biochemistry," said Ella, throwing the study text across the room, where it bounced off the wall and padded gently to the carpet. Study consoles are designed to take a lot of punishment.

"Don't let it get you down," I said, rather unhelpfully.

"It's easy for you to say, Marjory. It's not fair. It's like everyone else has been given a gift, but I'm still holding out my hand. I'm just not like you guys." She picked up the console and glared at it. "I hate biochem. I am so bad at it. I mean, what is the point of me even trying?"

"I thought you'd be good at biochemistry," I said, not thinking.

"Oh, yes, that would be so romantic wouldn't it? The poor girl with Metchnikoff Syndrome grows up to find the cure for her crippling disease."

"I'm sorry."

"No, I'm sorry. It's just that rumour going around school—it's getting me down."

Somebody had spread a rumour that Metchnikoff Syndrome was infectious. I thought I knew who had started that nasty bit of gossip.

"Just ignore the idiots. They're just jealous."

"It's not just at school, Marjory. I've had some hate mail, threats, that kind of thing."

"Oh, that's terrible."

"And Mum's really upset. The Knight Institute has asked me to undertake some clinical trials. Mum really wants me to go."

"The Knight Institute? That's in Sweden, isn't it? Your Mum can't force you to go, can she?"

"No, of course not, but she's really upset. I don't like to see her like that."

"I don't want you to change, Ella," I said softly.

"I'm sorry, Marjory. I know that you think I'm cool and all, but it's hard being me, when I could be so much better."

I held her in my arms.

"Don't change, Ella."

The time was right; we kissed.

❧

The next day Ella didn't come in to school. I immediately assumed it was something to do with me. I was so angry when I found out the real reason that I went to find Alicia and Jeddy.

They were in the majority common room, down-scanning copies of the latest college application hints, checking the social ratings and the projected salary estimates for all the trendiest universities.

"Oh my, look who it is," said Alicia. She made a big point of looking around the common room. "Where's your friend? Why aren't you trailing behind her, as per usual."

"You know where she is," I said. "You couldn't let her be, could you? You couldn't stand the thought that someone could be as nice as her without synths."

"I don't know what you're talking about," said Alicia.

"Ella has gone to Sweden to a medical research unit. She won't be at school for a long time, perhaps she'll never come back, and it's all thanks to you."

"Well, good," said Alicia. "Maybe they'll find a cure for her. We don't want the little freak about, do we, Jeddy?"

"Well, she was starting to dominate you, Marjory," said Jeddy. "We missed you. We're supposed to be your best friends."

"So, you decided to start a rumour that Metchnikoff Syndrome is infectious—which it isn't, by the way. You couldn't stand the fact that I liked her, could you?"

"You can't prove anything," said Alicia with a smirk.

"And I suppose you posted that nasty little rumour onto the global net?"

"Would I do a thing like that?" said Alicia.

"And thanks to you, some idiots threw a fire bomb though her window, last night."

Alicia turned as pale as ice, "What? Is she okay? Was anyone hurt?"

"They're fine. Their fire suppressor system took care of it. But because of you, her Mum and Dad have persuaded her that it will be best to get away for a while. Thank you, Alicia. Thanks a lot."

My phone rang. It played the sound of the CheeseDolls into the majority common room. I began to cry.

Jeddy said, "We didn't want to hurt her, Marjory. We didn't put the stuff onto the global net did we, Alicia?"

I looked at Alicia. I read the guilt written over her face.

"We used to be really good friends, Marjory." Alicia shrugged. "But it seems like you prefer the company of freaks."

❧

I took a week off school, pretending to be sick. I got a few disapproving messages from Mrs. McAllister's office, but I just ignored them.

I sat in front of the mirror—not my clickable mirror, but an old fashioned, glass mirror. I hadn't realized, that I was so, well, ugly. My once-perfect skin was blotchy; my hair had an unfortunate kink that caused it to curl up; my nose, well, the least said about my nose the better. Suffice it to say that it was no longer cute and button-like.

Choices, choices, there are so many choices in this life.

I had secluded myself in my suite while the changes took place. Mum screamed when I entered the family kitchen.

"What's happened to your face, darling," she said, rushing over. "You look terrible."

Father looked up from his paper and his face went notably whiter. "Is this some kind of majority rebellion thing, because I liked the old you," he said.

"This is the old me. I've taken out my click DNA."

"You've done what?" asked Mum, turning my face this way and that.

"Ack. Leave her be. She's age of majority, after all."

"I suppose so," said Mum. "At least nobody will see her, now she's not going to school."

"I will be attending school this morning," I said.

"No, absolutely not," said Mum.

"Leave her be," said Dad.

"I suppose this is all about Ella," said Mum.

I blushed, but said nothing, preserved my dignity, and made my way to school.

❧

I felt pretty nervous when I opened the door to school. I was expecting a whole lot of hassle. I walked along the corridor. Everyone ignored me. I saw them looking at me and turning away. It was as if I didn't exist. That was what it was like for Ella. If you didn't look perfect, you were nothing. It made me really angry.

I knew that there were a couple of people who could be relied on to say something.

"What have you done to yourself, Marjory?" asked Jeddy, when I walked into the majority common room.

"She's made herself look like her weirdo girlfriend," said Alicia.

All the other kids, all my so-called friends, started to laugh at me.

❧

It was an easy thing to do. I used the fabber in the school labs to knock up a special piece of click DNA. I used the same retrovirus technology that all click DNA uses, but instead of downloading it into a skin-patch I slipped it into a nice, off the shelf air-borne virus. I designed the virus with a limited lifespan and I designed it to be *very* infectious. As the template, I used some DNA excised from the follicle cells attached to a strand of Ella's hair.

I released the virus near the air vents. I imagined little bits of Ella floating though the school, landing on all the perfects students. I imagined the retrovirus snipping out bits of their DNA and pushing in something new and special.

I didn't know what was going to happen in the long-term. After all, the immune system is complex. Like Ella said, there are all kinds of bits and bobs working together. I did know that there were going to be some changes at the school. Ella's macrophages were incredibly efficient. Pretty soon, all my perfect looking friends were going to look a whole lot different.

❧

What do you know? It turned out that Metchnikoff Syndrome was contagious, after all.

There were geneticists crawling all over the Academy. They'd insisted on coming into the school to monitor us all. They were very interested in analyzing the results of my impromptu experiment.

Everybody suspected me. So what? They couldn't prove anything. I'd used Ella's ID when I fabbed the virus.

Ella would be back at school in a couple of weeks. She laughed her head off when I sent her the image of our class.

"Is that really what Alicia looks like?"

"Yep."

"Oh, wow." She studied the image I'd sent her: girls with acne, spectacles, frizzy hair, greasy hair, enormous noses or disappearing chins. "They look good," said Ella.

"They do look good," I said. In the faces of my friends, I could see an attractiveness that the sterility of click DNA beauty had taken away. We all looked good, and we all looked different.

I guess, it's true what they say: beauty is only gene deep.

The Forest in the Attic
L Lark

"The clearest way into the Universe is through a forest wilderness."
— John Muir

On his first night in the house on Whippoorwill Lane, Tsuki finds a forest hidden in his attic.

The house is old, pink and slanted left. It has been unoccupied for five decades, and they spend their first day pulling cobwebs from the door frames. By sunset, Tsuki and his mother have built a pile of weightless grey silk in the living room.

Upon arrival, they discover the previous tenants had left behind a number of personal relics; jars of buffalo nickels, stained inkwells, mismatched socks. The most numerous of these are the clocks— wall clocks, cuckoo clocks, alarm clocks that ring in anxious tones, reminding them of appointments they have no recollection of making.

Tsuki's mother takes them down, but hopeful about their value as antiques, piles them into the room adjacent to Tsuki's. They keep him awake through the night, arguing the hour amongst themselves.

"I'm going to order dinner. Go clean out the attic," Tsuki's mother tells him, brushing a cobweb from her sleeve. She is wearing old sweatpants, and her feet are coated by dust. She looks monochrome, like an old photograph.

The attic is a spacious room with a slanted ceiling, dominated by a fortress of boxes. Tsuki sets an empty garbage bag down and begins to work, collecting crumbling doilies, dried watercolour sets, broken teacups and several glass eyes. He sucks medicine from his inhaler, choked by gales of dust.

Tsuki descends to the bottom floor to eat wet, salty noodles out of a foam box, and then returns to the attic to finish breaking into the last locked trunk in the room's western corner.

The forest is inside.

It is disguised as what seems like a clunky pair of antique binoculars. Later, he will learn the object is a *stereoscope,* technology obsolete before he was born. Tsuki finds it wrapped in a blue peacoat, unaccompanied by note or instruction, and uses his shirtsleeve to wipe soot off its lenses. He coughs out a lungful of cobwebs, and holds the stereoscope to his eyes.

Suddenly, he is not in the attic at all.

There is snow on the ground. It fills the gaps between Tsuki's toes. He is surrounded by trees with black bark, so tall they harpoon into the bellies of clouds above. It had been sundown in the attic, but here it is night, and cold air makes Tsuki feel like he has been struck in the chest each time he inhales.

He listens for the chirp of an insect or the wail of an owl, but hears only relentless white noise. Tsuki nearly calls out, but pauses. A weak sound escapes his mouth, travelling no farther that his shadow.

He lowers the stereoscope, returning to the warm orange space of the attic. A vein throbs beneath his jawbone. Somewhere below, his mother calls for him to go to bed, but Tsuki stands frozen for a long moment, unsure of what to do.

He reviews the facts:

There is a forest in the attic.

The forest can only be seen through the stereoscope.

Tsuki had not been alone in the forest.

Just before returning, he had seen a trail of footprints in the snow, and they were not his own.

❧

In a way, Tsuki has been missing from the last six months of his life. His memories of the time are fluid, slippery, like the plot of a movie he'd seen while half-asleep. His father packing a suitcase, with a one-way ticket to Barcelona on his pillow. Divorce papers. A cross-country drive. A crumbling house that smells of mulch and old pennies. The unfamiliar skyline of pitched roofs through his window.

Tsuki and his mother arrived at the house on Whippoorwill Lane at the beginning of spring break. There is still a week and a half before Tsuki steps foot in his new high school. Aside from cleaning, he waits dully for time to pass, eating cold leftovers and thinking about the forest in the attic.

"You should look for a job. Plenty of places need part-time help," his mother says, watching Tsuki peel the crust off his second turkey sandwich. He hasn't built up the courage to look through the stereoscope again, and eating seems like a perfectly rational alternative.

Tsuki shrugs. His body is lanky, clattering, and his bones poke out like the appendages of a prehistoric beast. He looks younger than seventeen, especially in his oversize hoodies and loose jeans. People everywhere offer him food.

Tsuki yawns into his sleeve. The clocks in the next room had chimed all night, as if performing a melody they hadn't rehearsed. His mother watches him eat, frowning. They share black hair, fair skin and a wary skepticism of each other's motives.

"Can you at least finish unpacking your room today?" she says.

"After I finish the attic," Tsuki says with his mouth full.

She rolls her eyes and disappears, beating the dirt out of a welcome mat.

The attic is brighter at noon. Dust particles knock against his knees and hips, like panicked fireflies. Tsuki waves them aside with his hand and lowers to the edge of the trunk that contains the forest. He presses an ear against the lid, but hears only his own pulse.

In daylight, the stereoscope looks dull and unpolished. There is mint-green rust gathering at its edges. His thumb finds a letter inscribed beneath the stereoscope's left lens.

Q.

The forest is austere and uniform. Tsuki could be anywhere in the grid of black trees. It's snowing. There are blue spirals of light in gaps between the clouds, but other than that, the landscape is motionless.

"Hello?" he says again, feeling stupid. His teeth knock together painfully.

"Who are you? You're not supposed to be here," Tsuki hears from above him. The voice skips and crackles, as if transmitted through a shortwave radio. It is young, male, but Tsuki can't determine exactly where it's coming from. He turns the stereoscope up, and searches through the branches above him. Snow clouds the lenses, and after a moment Tsuki sees only a mosaic of grey patches.

"Shouldn't be here? I found this place in my attic."

There is a pause.

"That's impossible."

"Clearly not."

Tsuki hears a twig snap behind him and turns too quickly. For a moment, a slice of the attic is visible through the trees, like a curtain has been blown aside. It is dizzying, and Tsuki's left knee crumples.

The boy watches from between two trunks. He is Tsuki's age—seventeen, maybe eighteen—with auburn hair and eyes that look like ink splatter against the snow. Both hands are buried deeply in his coat pockets.

"Where did you find those?" the boy asks, nodding to the stereoscope pressed against Tsuki's brow. He is dressed in the sort of clothing found in history textbooks, accompanied by solemn descriptions of the Great Depression. His trousers are worn at the knee, and Tsuki can see the white bulge of the boy's big toe stabbing through his shoe.

"I found this forest in my attic. I don't know what these are, but I can't see here without them."

The boy's eyebrows jerk, as if he hadn't expected to be answered.

"Did my father send you?"

"Your father? No. I came here by accident."

The boy looks to each side, and wipes a stray eyelash from his cheek. There is a nervous twitch in the corner of his mouth. Tsuki stares at the pink skin over his cheekbones for a moment too long.

"In that case, I don't think you should stay. It's always watching. It'll probably be cross that I'm talking to you."

"What will?"

"The thing in the trees. Where did you say you'd come from?"

Tsuki looks up, but sees nothing aside from an occasional pulse of blue light, and branches sagging beneath snow. Droplets of cold water gather in the corners of his eyes.

"Don't look for it," the boy says, grabbing ahold of Tsuki's wrist. The contact is unexpected, and it knocks the stereoscope from Tsuki's face.

Suddenly, he is back in the attic. The light, which had once bisected his waist, now wallows by his ankles. He'd spent only a few minutes in the forest, but it appears much more time has passed here.

He can hear his mother's voice calling his name from the landing. The attic smells like frying oil.

"I'm—I'll be right there," he shouts. Tsuki feels shell-shocked, battered, like he's woken from a dream of falling at the exact moment of impact. He is still holding the stereoscope, but his hands are trembling.

Tsuki rewraps the stereoscope in the peacoat, and pushes it to the bottom of the trunk. He tries very hard not to think about the boy in the forest, and his pink cheeks, and the grey of snow melting in dark hair. He tries not to think about the evenly spaced trees, or the thing living in their branches.

In his rush to leave the room, he does not notice the lime-green shoots curling out between floorboards.

❧

The next morning, Tsuki pulls a sweater and scarf from an unpacked box. They smell old and frail, but so does everything in the house. He is too afraid to lean against the walls, lest they snap and crumble. The plumbing holds conversations about the temperature, while the clocks in the next room debate the time.

"Where are you going?" Tsuki's mother asks, looking up from her laptop as he tries to sneak past. She has already memorized which floor panels whine beneath a footstep.

"I was going to look for a job."

She gives an unconvinced stare, blowing a strand of hair from her eyes.

"I'll be back soon," he assures her, and steps outside for the first time in days. The fresh air makes him lightheaded. For a moment, Tsuki has to lean against the porch swing, waiting for his eyes to accept the sunlight.

Tsuki's phone tells him there is a library eleven blocks away. He pulls his hood up against the rain, and stares at the sidewalk. The asphalt is uneven, conquered by roots breaking out from the earth. The sky is the colour of tarnished silver.

Tsuki ignores the librarian's offer for help, and finds the town's archives in the basement. It is a modern building with florescent lighting. The only embellishments are the lampposts that light the stairway to the basement. They are bronze and shaped like antlers, stabbing into the darkness.

The basement is stark and well organized, with a collection of digitized newspapers on an unoccupied computer. Tsuki searches through the town's records during the house's early years, but finds little of interest, aside from the outbreak of Spanish Flu in 1918. It takes two hours of scanning through obituaries to find a few names of interest.

There is one that stands out more than the others.

Quentin Thorpe, age 18, died in his family home.

There is no cause of death given, but Tsuki traces the Q on the screen with his index finger. Further search on Quentin Thorpe yields nothing, aside from a brief mention in a newspaper article, citing him as the champion in a 100-yard dash. Quentin's mother was a seamstress. His father taught science at a local university. Neither one gives a statement about their son's death.

Tsuki prints the article out, and stuffs it into his pocket. He leaves the building with his hood pulled over his eyes, ignoring the librarian's request that he sign up for a card.

His mother is not home when he gets back, but there is a cold bowl of pasta in the fridge. Tsuki microwaves a portion, watching it spin in the radioactive light behind the glass door, but cannot bring himself to eat. The forest is waiting upstairs. More importantly, there is a dead boy waiting upstairs. And possibly something else, but Tsuki isn't ready to think about that yet.

He stops by the guest room on his way to the attic and grabs the clock whose numbers most closely match those on his phone. The space is filled with frantic ticking, like time has tripped and splattered across the floor. Tsuki closes the door on the way out.

The attic is dim, aside from a chute of yellow light falling in from the window. It illuminates the cluster of young plants, wiggling their way out of the floor. *It's an old house,* Tsuki thinks. *Things like this must happen.* But something makes him want to crush the shoots beneath his boot.

"You shouldn't be here," he tells them, searching for the stereoscope amongst the crumbling clothing in the trunk. The plants answer by growing two inches while he watches.

Tsuki notes the time before pressing the stereoscope to his eyes. It is four in the afternoon. The ticking marks seconds like a countdown.

The boy is waiting for him, leaning against a tree with his arms crossed. His shoulders are sagging and shapeless, as if he has been standing for too long. This time, Tsuki is calm enough to take inventory of the boy's features. He has a long nose and enormous knuckles. His eyes are wide, with yawning pupils that stare at Tsuki in the way a galaxy might stare at a small creature, scuttling on a rock. Tsuki is afraid, and not entirely sure why he wants to reach out and feel the ridge of bone above the boy's eyebrow.

"You're back," the boy says, without inflection.

"Yes. I had to ask—"

"You shouldn't have come back. It's looking for you. It's upset that you're here."

"—are you Quentin Thorpe?"

The boy uncrosses his arms. The left corner of his mouth twitches.

"Be quiet. It's always listening."

Tsuki exhales the first syllable of a word, but the boy reaches out and takes a firm hold on his wrist, compressing the vein that leads to Tsuki's palm. Tsuki's fingers seize, but he follows the boy's gaze up to the net of branches above them.

The trees are swaying. The boy gives his arm a tug, and Tsuki struggles not to let the stereoscope slip.

"What is it?"

"Don't talk. Come with me."

The boy pulls Tsuki at a pace that makes him fear his knees are going to snap apart. The boy runs without panting, while Tsuki struggles for every breath, uselessly attempting to stop as the boy drags him through the trees.

"Wait," he finally gasps. "I can't."

Tsuki can't recall which direction they'd run, but it hardly matters. Wherever in the forest the boy has led him, it is identical from where they came. His brain struggles with infinite repetition, inserting shadows and movement where there are none. Tsuki feels like he's spun in place for too long.

"We have to keep going," the boy says, without breaking the connection between them. Tsuki can feel his pulse knocking against the boy's fingertips. He needs a puff from his inhaler, but he can't take his hand away from the stereoscope.

"I can't. What are we running from? What is this place?"

A branch shatters, and splinters tumble from the canopy. It takes Tsuki a moment to realize what is so odd about the sight of the crouched silhouette above them. He sees it only when he blinks, imprinted like a burn on his memory. Its eyes glow with lunar brilliance. Tsuki can make out long arms with enormous, angular elbows, and a mouth that shines with fresh saliva.

"It's too late," the boy whispers, releasing Tsuki's hand. "It saw you."

"Are you Quentin?" Tsuki says, which is not what he wants to ask, but there is a rumble in his ears. It is either coming from the monster or from his heart, rattling loose beneath his breastplate.

"Ask me again later," the boy says, and knocks the stereoscope out of Tsuki's hands.

It goes tumbling to the attic floor, and Tsuki scrambles after it, disoriented by the sudden change in temperature and location. He trips over something while reaching for the stereoscope, and hits the floor knee-first. The aftershock races up his thigh like an electrical impulse.

When Tsuki looks back, it takes him a moment to decide whether or not he is hallucinating. The plants have been replaced by—or rather, grown into—a small group of trees with roots that spread across the floorboards. Tsuki recognizes the species. He has just been standing amidst a grove of them, with a boy who is both dead and not.

His fingers fumble, but he manages to lift the stereoscope and return to the forest. It is empty again, and the snow is falling without urgency, gathering in Tsuki's eyelashes and collar. He is too afraid to call for Quentin, but stands still for a long moment, staring into the blackness between trunks.

Eventually, he returns to the attic, where the trees are pushing against the ceiling. The room is filled with violet light. Tsuki glances at the wall clock he'd brought up from downstairs, and sees that three hours have passed since his initial journey into the forest.

As he returns the stereoscope to the trunk, Tsuki finds a leather portfolio filled with notes and esoteric symbols, labeled by impossibly long numbers. The handwriting is small and manic. Tsuki understands little of what is written, but he tucks the portfolio into his waistband.

He can hear his mother sneezing downstairs. The mould in the walls gives her allergies. Tsuki does not think she'll react well to the forest threatening to break through her attic. He locks the door, pockets the key, only noticing the collection of new shoots peeking out of the floorboards as he closes the door behind him.

❧

Tsuki accompanies his mother into town the next day. He stands behind her in the checkout line at the grocery store, thirsty and bored, staring into the florescent beams. He waits in the lobby at the dentist's office, flipping through a fashion magazine while thinking of Quentin's shell-like cheekbones. He watches droplets scramble up the windshield at the carwash, while his mother taps her fingernails against the steering wheel.

Tsuki is distracted. He lets long moments lapse before answering her questions. He jumps when she pokes her finger into his shoulder.

"What is wrong with you?" she asks, biting the straw to her smoothie. Tsuki's mother chews her pens, her fingernails, salty chopsticks from Chinese takeout. She watches him over the rim of her cup, while two enormous fans batter the car with hot air.

Tsuki thinks about the forest in the attic, and the trees breaking through their floorboards, and the monster concealed in the canopy, and what he says is, "Nothing. I'm fine."

She gives him a doubting look, but does not press further. Tsuki and his mother are close in wordless ways—they share meaningful glances and gestures, but conversations often fail them. She drives them home in silence, while Tsuki watches clouds churning around the hills on the horizon.

"I'm going to go read," he says when they get home, climbing the stairs before she can respond. Tsuki hears her exhale and close her office door.

In the attic, the trees have grown. There are six now, hunkered beneath the ceiling, and another eight in various states of maturity. Tsuki has to shove through branches to get to the trunk where the stereoscope is hidden. A splinter throbs dully in his left elbow.

This time, Tsuki pulls on a sweater and a pair of wool gloves he finds in the trunk. They itch and smell of someone else's skin. Auburn hairs are ensnared in the fabric.

Quentin isn't waiting for him in the forest. The snowfall is fresh, buoyant and undisturbed. Tsuki inhales, searching for the mildewed scent of Quentin's clothes, but finds only the clean aroma of icicles dripping from a tree branch.

"Hello?" Tsuki calls.

"Quiet," Quentin says, from somewhere behind his left ear. "It already knows you're here."

Tsuki turns, and finds Quentin crouched beneath a tree branch, swatting pine needles from his eyes. The skin over Quentin's face is tight, grey and translucent. He coughs into the crook of his elbow. Suddenly, Tsuki realizes that Quentin has always looked sick. Tsuki just hasn't noticed because Quentin's eyes are reflective and clear, the color of darkness around a bare light bulb.

"I had to see you," Tsuki says, simultaneous to the realization that this statement is true. It was not the forest that hummed to Tsuki in the night, sneaking into the lulls between clock chimes. It was the memory of Quentin's slender hands and peculiar expression.

"You have to stop. It doesn't want you here."

"What is this place?"

"It's a forest, obviously. My father made it for me, and you don't belong here," Quentin says, and turns to disappear into the trees. Tsuki scrambles after him, half-collapsing into the snow.

"You're Quentin Thorpe. You're dead."

"Dead? What are you talking about? Obviously, I'm not dead. I'm here, aren't I?"

Tsuki doesn't immediately respond to that. He follows the trail of Quentin's footprints in the snow, trying to keep his breathing steady. There is something about the forest that reminds Tsuki of travelling through high-altitudes, searching for stray molecules of oxygen.

"Well, maybe I died," Quentin amends, finally turning to meet Tsuki. The warmth of Quentin's breath crosses the distance between them. "My father brought me here to wait while he searched for a cure, but that doesn't mean it's safe for you. Please, go."

Tsuki doesn't put the stereoscope down. He focuses the lenses on Quentin's mouth, gnawing on the translucent nail over his index finger.

"How did you find this place?" Quentin says, seemingly coming to accept that Tsuki is not leaving.

"It was in my attic."

"It's my attic."

"Not anymore. What year do you think it is?"

"I don't know. 1918? 1919? I can't have been here longer than a month."

Tsuki doesn't answer that, and by the time he opens his mouth to change the subject, he notices Quentin is staring at the empty space over his shoulder.

"Should I run?" Tsuki asks, with an odd pressure in his diaphragm.

"Yes," Quentin says, and they both set off.

Tsuki can't keep up, but he follows Quentin's streaming shadow. The forest passes in alternating streaks of white and grey. Tsuki hears a steady huff behind him. It does not seem to gain ground or fall behind, but Tsuki can't bring himself to pause and look.

Eventually, Quentin stops and allows Tsuki to tip forward, breathing into his cupped palms. Tsuki's lungs won't inflate. His brain has run through its oxygen, and he isn't sure if he is imagining the dull blue light on the far horizon.

"We can't go any farther. The forest stops. It won't come any closer to the edge. It's afraid of the blue light."

"What is that thing?"

"My father put it here. It was supposed to keep me safe, but I think it's starting to get hungry."

Tsuki watches Quentin's bare-bulb eyes, sweeping the horizon.

"What is this place? Why is it in my attic?"

"I told you, it's *my* attic. I'm just waiting until my father comes to get me. You shouldn't come back here anymore. It knows you now. It'll be waiting."

Tsuki thinks he hears rustling in the tree branches, but his eyes follow the arrows of Quentin's collarbones to the delicate scoop at the base of his throat. Tsuki reaches out and tugs the hem of Quentin's sleeve.

"What are you doing?" Quentin says, looking down at Tsuki's blue fingertips. His mouth slides into an odd frown that Tsuki would laugh at, if he were not so terrified.

"Nothing. I'm dizzy. I don't understand this place."

"You'll get hurt if you stay. Please, go," Quentin says, with such sincerity and sadness that Tsuki lowers the stereoscope, immediately struck by the absence of Quentin's slender neck and immense eyes.

❧

Tsuki is not surprised to find the trees waiting when he returns. They take up nearly all the floor space, whining as they strain to grow against the ceiling. Tsuki feels a rare emotion—something between exhilaration and fear—that he normally keeps locked in a small chamber beneath his heart. He has to climb over roots and low-hanging branches to reach the attic door, ignoring splinters that slip into the skin of his palms and fingertips.

He does not want to have to explain this to his mother.

"What the hell have you being doing?" she asks, when Tsuki descends the stairs, pinching the bridge of his nose. He has a headache, and there is a tedious throb in his stomach, like he hasn't eaten in days.

"I was taking a nap," he says. She rolls her eyes at him.

They eat in front of the television. His mother hasn't hooked up the cable yet; they watch a conspiracy talk show on a local network, spearing macaroni with plastic forks. Every time Tsuki inhales, he catches the spiced scent of pine seeping down from above them.

"Are you okay? We can talk, you know. About your father, even," she says after, forearms buried beneath yellow suds in the kitchen sink. Tsuki dries the dishes with a striped towel, listening for the moment roots finally break through the ceiling.

"What? No. I'm all right," he says, and doesn't add *except for the dead boy, and the monster, and the forest in the attic.* Tsuki takes a puff from his inhaler. "I'm going to go back upstairs."

"What have you been doing up there?" she says. His mother wipes her forehead with the back of her wrist. A bubble of soap wiggles on her left temple.

Tsuki hears something thump from the floor above.

"I've been tired lately. Maybe I'm getting a cold," he says, and fakes a cough on his trek up the stairs. For a moment, Tsuki forgets he isn't

79

really sick, and the congestion in his chest is anxiety, building like plaque. There is a steady creaking coming from above him, like trees fighting each other for space.

There is another noise too, something low that rattles Tsuki's eardrum. He thinks he's heard it before, but cannot recall if it was in reality or in dreams. Tsuki's hand hovers over the attic's doorknob for too long, waiting for the sound to recede, but it doesn't.

He opens the door, and finds a forest waiting behind it.

It is not the vast, uniform forest Tsuki's sees behind the stereoscope. The trees are cramped, twisted, like contortionists vying for space on a small stage. The attic smells like rotting wood, but the air tastes faintly of cinnamon. It tickles the hairs in Tsuki's nostrils, and he sneezes into the crook of his arm.

Tsuki climbs through the forest, shoving aside cardboard boxes and leather suitcases that have been disturbed by the roots in the floorboards. The trunk that holds the stereoscope has been tipped over, and clothes lay twisted across the floor. The stereoscope itself is half-concealed by the blue peacoat. Tsuki reaches for it, but doesn't lift it to his eyes.

He is quite certain about it now.

There is something in the attic with him.

Leaves shift in the room's opposite corner. Tsuki thinks he sees damp, orange orbs blinking between branches. He takes a careful step towards the attic door, and the eyes—if they are eyes—follow the motion of his ankle with great interest.

"Tsuki," his mother says from across the door. He sees the knob give a perfunctory clockwise twist, but go no farther.

"What are you doing up here?" she calls through the door. Tsuki wonders if she can hear the low rumble the creature gives as it shifts in the mesh of branches. Tsuki wonders what she'll say when she sees he's allowed a forest to grow in their attic. Tsuki wonders if he's about to be eaten. Tsuki wonders if being eaten is the better option.

"I'm just reading."

"In the attic? In the dark?"

"It's atmospheric," he says, stepping carefully over the roots, keeping his eyes on the silhouette of the creature across the room. It hasn't moved, other than to tilt its head with canine curiosity, and flicker each time Tsuki blinks, as if it exists only in alternate milliseconds.

"You'll go blind. Do you want me to bring you a lamp?"

"I'm fine," Tsuki says. Somewhere in the attic, the wall clock marks the moments until Tsuki is murdered or grounded for six months or engulfed by the swelling branches of the trees around him. He feels his mother release her hold on the doorknob, and take a hesitant step back on the landing.

Go, he pleads silently, while the monster watches with happy, hungry eyes.

"Okay," she says finally. Tsuki listens to her take agonizingly slow steps down the stairs, while the creature ambles towards him.

He takes off towards the door, but the roots are thick and snapped like broken bones. Tsuki tumbles, falling knee-first into the hollow between trunks. He waits silently in the dark, listening to the drawling breath of the creature in the tree above him.

There is a strip of yellow light beneath the attic door. He pulls himself over the next root, trying to suppress a panicked wheeze. His knee is wet, and Tsuki is certain he is bleeding. He briefly wonders if interdimensional creatures have a keen sense of smell. A stray leaf lands by Tsuki's ear, and his jaw clenches.

Something—not a leaf this time, definitely not a leaf—strokes the ticklish curve of Tsuki's heel. When it touches him, Tsuki's mind suddenly floods with memories he isn't sure are his. He watches his own infant toes, wiggling in a shaft of sunlight. He sees his mother twirling in a poppy-red dress, while his father takes photographs with a Polaroid camera. He recalls the first sentence he ever spoke aloud, in a hesitant mixture of English and Japanese.

Tsuki thinks he is going to scream. His mouth pops open, but another sound tunnels through the forest. It is the ring of an alarm sounding from the wall clock.

The claw at Tsuki's face draws back, and he moves without thought, scrambling for the sliver of light. He makes it to the door, but his hand flounders with the knob.

The alarm rings, and the creature wails like a car alarm in reverse. For a moment, Tsuki cannot be sure if he has been in the attic for thirty seconds or thirty years, and when he finally stumbles from the room, he half-expects to find the house crumbling with age after his absence.

It is not, but Tsuki feels an odd stiffness in his limbs, like he has been standing still for decades, muscles swelling with adrenaline, heart trapped between beats for lengths of time unknown.

❧

Tsuki brings three of the clocks into his bedroom. Their mismatched chatter is somehow comforting.

Tsuki tries the stereoscope in his room, but sees nothing aside from a faint blue glow in all directions. Frustrated, he drops the stereoscope to the nightstand, and stares at it for a long time, trying to decipher if the sounds he hears are the clocks in the next room or claws clicking down the hallway. Twice, he gets up to check on his mother, twisting uneasily beneath white sheets.

When Tsuki sleeps, he is not surprised to find himself in the forest. Quentin is waiting for him, wavering in his peripheral vision. Tsuki cannot tell if Quentin is a boy, or an owl, or a snowflake, or a moment, but he is beautiful and awash in pale blue light.

"It's not that the clocks don't work. It's that they do," Tsuki says, suddenly grasping something that had alluded him before.

"I told you not to come back. The forest exists in time. You gave it space. You'll never be safe now."

"Who are you?" Tsuki asks, even though he knows. This boy is Quentin Thorpe, deceased. He has lived in Tsuki's attic for almost a hundred years. He may or may not exist, but his eyes are like radiant orbs in the darkness. Tsuki reaches out and touches the protruding bone at Quentin's left wrist.

"Don't," Quentin says. "It'll never stop growing. You have to give it time or space, and you only have so much of the latter."

"What do I do?" Tsuki asks, moving into the bubble of Quentin's warmth. Quentin does not back away, but he frowns at the sight of Tsuki's thumb mapping the topography of veins on the back of his hand.

"I have no idea," Quentin admits. "I just live here. Or am dead here, I'm not entirely sure anymore. My father must have left notes."

"He did. I don't understand them, and now there's a monster in my attic."

"It's not sure how to move in space. It'll be slow for now, but it'll learn. I wouldn't hesitate. It's probably pretty hungry by now. Wake up, Tsuki."

Tsuki does, reeling like he's been struck in the back of the head with no warning. Tsuki cannot recall whether or not he'd told Quentin his name, but Quentin's pronunciation had been precise and his pink tongue darted out slightly between syllables.

The house is groaning. In the darkness, Tsuki imagines his bedroom ceiling dipping beneath the weight of the forest overhead. He searches for a flashlight in a duffle bag of camping equipment, while his heart synchronizes with the rhythm of clocks in the next room.

He builds a nest out of throw pillows, and tries to make sense of the papers in the leather portfolio. The text weaves through itself, occasionally in spirals of shrinking handwriting. The pages are a mess of English, German and Latin. At times, language fails altogether, and the sheets fill with overlapping geometric diagrams.

"I don't know, Quentin," he says aloud, although he is sure they are separated by something more substantial than space. He occasionally glances through the stereoscope, watching the pulse of blue light and searching for the familiar sweep of Quentin's hair.

It is when Tsuki looks through the stereoscope at the notes on his bed that he understands. In their place is a clock in a wooden frame with multiple hands that loop in both directions. It ticks at each half second, sounding strangely desperate. At the clock's centre, the letter Q is engraved in delicate script. Tsuki reaches for it, but his hand stops short. There is an odd sensation, like breath against his fingertips.

"Where did you find it? My father built that while I was sick. If you break it, I'll probably die. Again, anyway," says a voice, from every point in the vast blue void.

"The clocks are keeping time. They're literally *keeping* time. That's what the forest is, isn't it? It's not a place. It's a moment."

For an instant, Tsuki thinks he sees the misty silhouette of Quentin, struggling to form.

"How long have I actually been here?" Quentin says, briefly appearing and then dissolving.

"Almost a hundred years," Tsuki says, splaying his fingers into the mist. He wonders if Quentin's consciousness is weaving between them. There are other things Tsuki wants to say, but the words are dangerous and stuck in his throat, like a wolf squirming in a hunter's trap.

"You should do it. The forest won't stop growing if you don't."

"I want to see you," Tsuki says, ignoring Quentin's last statement.

"Then bring the clock to the attic. Be careful. The creature will be waiting for you."

"What is that thing?"

"They don't have names. They are all the things you've forgotten. And they're very, very angry about it. Go. Before it gets any faster."

Tsuki lowers the stereoscope, dizzy from the transition between worlds, and gathers the papers strewn across his bed. He puts on a coat, scarf and a pair of heavy wool socks. Tsuki also finds a baseball bat, hidden beneath a dirty pair of jeans in his unpacked luggage.

❧

The forest is climbing down the stairs. The forest is expanding into the hallways. The forest has broken through the windows on the second floor, and an owl sways predatorily in the canopy. A long branch winds into his mother's room, stopping just before it reaches her puffed cheek. In her sleep, she murmurs in strained Japanese. The room smells faintly of vanilla candlewax.

"Really?" Tsuki mutters, and begins to push his way through. The trek up the stairs is long and exhausting. Tsuki grips the flashlight in one hand and the baseball bat in the other, struggling to maintain balance over newly uneven terrain.

The attic door has been shattered, but the forest is silent. If the creature is hidden somewhere above him, then it is resting or bidding its time. Tsuki enters, and lifts the stereoscope, again finding himself in the forest where snow drifts from a vortex of blue clouds.

"Quentin," he calls. The pine trees roar in the wind, and the clock ticks happily in response, like a lost pet reunited with its owner. Quentin is sitting in the dip of a low branch, watching his feet swing. He does not look up when Tsuki approaches, so Tsuki slides his palm over Quentin's thigh and presses into the muscle with unnecessary force.

"I brought the clock," Tsuki tries.

"Destroy it now. You give the forest more space every time you come here, and the creature could be anywhere by now."

"No."

Quentin moves with unexpected urgency, and presses his mouth to the stretch of Tsuki's forehead. His lips are feverishly hot and singe Tsuki's skin.

"It's fine, really. I've died before. It's not so bad. More boring than anything."

"You do it," Tsuki says, attempting to push the clock into Quentin's arms. It falls, landing face-up in the snow, while its hands whirl wildly across the numbers.

"I can't. Do it now before I lose my nerve, or you get eaten."

As if called, a long shadow passes over them, but Tsuki cannot bring himself to look. He takes a step forward, raising the baseball bat. Tsuki's eyelashes fill with snow, and his vision floods with colourless light.

He brings the bat down on the clock, and hears glass shattering. For a moment, the world feels like it's been tipped on its axis. Snow drifts horizontally across Tsuki's vision. Trees shoot out from the ground at angles, falling against each other with resounding crashes. Tsuki struggles to keep the stereoscope at his eyes, while he tumbles to the ground.

Then, it is over. The forest is still, and Quentin is staring down at the shattered gears by his feet. The creature, crouched in a nearby tree, blinks each eye slowly.

"You're still here," Tsuki says, propping himself up on splintered, aching elbows.

"So are you."

"Did it work?" Tsuki asks, but hesitates before lowering the stereoscope, unsure of what he will find in the attic. He blinks the snow out of his eyes, and finds that he is still in the forest, in Quentin's forest, staring at Quentin's knobby hands with his own eyes for the first time.

"You're still here," Tsuki says again. He lifts the stereoscope to his face and down again. The forest is still there, and it is still snowing, and Quentin is staring at him like a tree starved for sunlight.

"Why can't I—" Tsuki begins, and cannot finish. Tsuki feels like his tongue is engorged, like his pupils are swelling. He has come to the edge of a realization, but can push himself no further.

"You gave the forest time," Quentin says, while quiet laughter sputters out of his mouth. Quentin doubles over and clutches his torso, like he is manually holding his own body together.

"What are you talking about?" Tsuki says. He tries the stereoscope again and again, but the landscape never changes.

"You gave it your time," Quentin says, and when he looks up again, Tsuki can see his eyes. They are black and immense, and Tsuki is terrified and perhaps slightly in love. The creature, forgotten, watches from the branches with twitching fingers.

"I have to go back home," Tsuki whispers, even as the trees seem to lean in to welcome him. Quentin laughs, and reaches out for Tsuki's shoulders, with a look of relief in his eyes. He smiles like a fissure in an enormous fault line.

"I don't think you understand," Quentin says, and curls his fingers into the spaces between Tsuki's vertebrae. "You gave it *your* time."

Tsuki lets the stereoscope drop sideways to the ground. He feels something being pulled from his solar plexus, like an unraveling string. Time escapes from the cavities in his nose and mouth, while

Quentin holds him up, whispering into his hair, and the creature watches from the trees, sated and bored.

In the forest, in the attic, in the house on Whippoorwill Lane, the snow falls and falls.

Enough Time

Christopher E Long

I stir under my heavy comforter and glance at the digital clock out of habit. But the clock is lifeless. All utilities stopped running five days ago. Water. Gas. Power. The people we'd all taken for granted to keep these things working apparently decided that they didn't want to spend the last few days of their lives at work. Not having a working refrigerator is inconvenient, but for the past five days my father and I have barely mustered anything that resembles an appetite. But when we do, we eat non-perishable food, like cereal and pasta. It's kind of funny that my father, who'd been a strict proponent of a low-carbohydrate lifestyle, now only eats carbs. It had been wreaking havoc on his digestive tract, but after a few loud farts, he seemed to be fine. It would be nice for the phones to work, but at this point, I wouldn't even know what to say to my friends. There's not a lot to say.

I get up and pull aside the curtains and peer out through the window. It's a sunny and warm spring day. It's days like this where there are limitless possibilities. Some of my fondest memories occurred on days like this. Ditching school when I was a sophomore and going to the beach where Lance asked me to junior prom. Or the one time during my freshman year my dad and I played hooky, spending the sunny day together at Disneyland. And who could forget that prefect April day three years ago when, on a day a lot like this, I laughed for the first time since my mother died. My father had let me drive the car. I didn't even have my learners permit. But with the top down on the '68 Mustang, he let me drive to school. We laughed the whole way there. I'm pretty sure I damaged the transmission, but my father didn't seem to mind.

In spite of myself, a smile spreads across my face thinking about that day. For the briefest of moments, I get a twinge of an emotion from before the news—hope. But like a flame flickering on a windy day, the emotion is extinguished because the reality of the hopeless situation crashes down on me. It seems like the slow march toward our destruction makes it harder and harder to remember the good days. With only a week left, memories of better days are elusive and fleeting. It's like I have Alzheimer's and there's a permanent fog that clouds my memory.

I suddenly get the feeling that I'm being watched. I look around outside. My gaze finally lands on the person standing at the second floor window of the Griffith's house. It's Jude. Jude the Obscure, at least that's what everyone at school called him. It seems like every high school has someone like him. Someone quiet and brooding. Dark. Morose. Jude could always be found on the outskirts, hovering just on the periphery, but often when I turned to look at him, he'd be gone, as if I'd imagined him. He's always been around, but I knew nothing about him. When our neighbours the Griffith's packed up their car to travel east to die with family, Jude had moved into the abandoned house. I never saw him coming or going, but just caught glimpses of him from time to time.

Feeling self-conscience for staring at him through the window, I raise my hand and wave. He doesn't wave back. It's then that I notice the rose resting on the windowsill. It wasn't there before. I would've noticed it. It appears to have been freshly picked. There's condensation on the red petals. The bottom of the stem is jagged and knobby, obviously torn from the bush, not clipped. Peering out through the window again, I glance at the Griffith's rose bush in their front yard. My eyes drift up to the upstairs window, but Jude is no longer there.

I set the rose on the bathroom counter and stare at my reflection. My hair is a tangled mess, and I've got dark circles under my eyes. I turn to the side and stare at my profile. I've probably lost fifteen pounds in the last month. If I would've known how much weight I would lose eating nothing but canned foods, I would've saved myself countless stomach aches from Mrs. Crawford, the cheerleading faculty advisor, who submitted us to her "jiggle test" every Monday morning. If there was the slightest jiggle, she'd put us on a liquid diet that week. I'd make myself sick over the weekend to make sure I made weight. Seems really stupid now that I ever got so worked up over something as trivial as that. Today I'm just grateful that there are five more cans of pears. If I work really hard, I might be able to stretch out the canned pears until the end. It's not much, but those pears are pretty much all I've got going right now.

Heading downstairs, I find my father sitting on the living room floor with a swathe of photos spread out all around him, almost blanketing the carpet. He hasn't shaved in I don't know how long. "Hey, Pop," I say.

His eyes are bloodshot, glassy and unfocused. "Hey, Brenda."

"When's the last time you got any sleep?"

He shrugs.

"You need to sleep. You look horrible."

He dismisses me with a wave. "I'll get all the rest I need soon." Perhaps recognizing the callousness of his words, my father appears to struggle with the right thing to say, but he finally gives up and turns his attention once again to the photos. "Come look at this," he says.

I look down at the picture. I've never seen it before. It's a photo of the front of our house. My parents pose next to a Sold realtor sign. My father playfully grimaces as he holds my very pregnant mother in both arms, struggling to support the weight of his wife and their unborn child. "Your mother was about ready to pop," he says. "You were born three days after this picture was taken."

My mother was so beautiful. She glowed. Makeup or no makeup, dressed to impress or wearing grubbies, she was a stunner, a natural beauty.

My father rubs his eyes. "Man, I miss her. Hopefully, we'll be seeing her shortly."

"Is that what you believe?" I ask. "That we'll be reunited after we die?"

My father shrugs and sifts through the stack of photos. "I don't know, Brenda. I just don't know. It's a nice idea of a friendly face waiting for us on the other side."

Many people are grappling with their spiritual beliefs. I suppose that's natural because the world as we know it is going to end, that much is sure. All the leading scientists agree. While there's still disagreement on the chances of survival for various bugs and aquatic life, it is widely acknowledged that humans are not going to escape total annihilation. Ever since the asteroid became public, religious fervour had spread. Church attendance soared. Sects that were on the fringe suddenly became legitimate. A rash of suicide cults was organizing public rituals where thousands of followers killed themselves. Every wacko with a means to communicate their nutty religious messages had more followers than they knew what to do with. I guess that was something positive about losing electricity—the news coverage of all these freaks stopped.

I stare at the photograph of my parents. A neighbourhood block party is going on in the background. Tables and chairs are set up in the middle of the street, and men and women mill about, drinking beer and eating barbecue. A group of children play with a hose, dousing each other with water. An image of someone milling about in a crowd by a table catches my attention. At first I don't even know why my eyes linger on him. There's nothing remarkable about the guy. Nothing immediately stands out. He wears a white T-shirt and shorts. His hair is slightly long and unkempt. My brain tries to make sense of it. In a flash, it dawns on me. "When was this picture taken?" I ask.

"A few days before you were born, so '97."

I hold the picture up so my father can see it and point to the image of the guy in question. "If this was taken in '97, then who is this?"

Squinting, my father stares at the picture. "I can't see who you mean."

"It's the spitting image of a guy I go to school with," I say. "Jude the Obscure."

"Jude the who?"

"Jude Simon. He just moved in next door."

"You mean the kid in the Griffith's place?"

"Yeah."

My father scoffs and the closest thing to a smile that I've seen on his face in weeks appears. "There's no way that's him. Probably his father or something."

"It looks just like him."

My father gently sets the photo down on top of the others. He looks around the floor, like a general surveying his troops on a battlefield, trying to strategize the next move.

"Do you think we have enough food and water?" I ask. "The water in the bathtub is pretty low."

"To last five more days?"

"Yeah."

He chuckles, but it's humourless. "I think we're okay, but what's the difference anyway? We're going to die one way or the other."

I bristle, and say, "Yeah, I guess, but—"

I'm cut off by a deafening explosion. The entire house shakes like a treetop in a breeze, and I can feel waves rolling across the floor like the tide. My father jumps to his feet and runs to the stairs, bounding up them two at a time. I chase after him, following him into the master bedroom. He opens the sliding door and we go out to the balcony that overlooks the backyard and the ravine just on the other side of the fence. Off in the distance, a massive cloud of debris and dust billows into the air.

A fiery ball streaks across the sky and plummets into the Earth. I feel the impact more than hear it. The shockwave smacks us like a truck, knocking me off my feet and sending me flying into the stucco wall. The glass on the sliding door shatters and rains down on the floor in my father's room.

My father bends down next to me. He has black soot on his face and blood oozes from his nose. His lips move but I can't hear what he says. He gets close to my ear and, like I'm in a long tunnel with him at the other side, I hear, "Are. You. Okay?"

I nod my head yes.

He helps me to my feet. My legs feel wobbly and I stumble, nearly falling, but he holds me up. Dozens of fiery balls streak across the sky. I don't know how long we stand there on the balcony and watch the destruction rain down. The scientists warned that a series of smaller asteroids would enter the atmosphere nearly a week before the larger humanity-killer, like heralds signally the impending arrival of their lord.

The loud ringing in my ears subsides, and I hear my father say, "This is how it begins."

Movement below attracts my attention. Jude stands in our yard and stares up at me. "Are you okay?" he asks.

I nod my head yes.

My father glances down at the boy. "Hey."

"Hey," Jude says.

"Are you okay?"

Jude motions to me, and says, "I was checking to make sure Brenda was okay."

My father nods his head, then turns and disappears inside his room, the crunching sound of glass under his slippers.

Jude and I stand there a moment, the silence stretching on and on, until finally I say, "Are you all alone in the Griffith's house?"

He nods his head, looking down at his feet, as if embarrassed by this fact.

I don't know what else to say, and maybe there really isn't anything left to say. "Well, take care."

"You, too."

I disappear inside the house.

❧

The next night I crawl out my bedroom window with a sleeping bag and make my way to the roof. Zipping myself inside the bag, I stare up at the sky. The asteroid is just barely visible in the horizon. It surprises me that it's less than four days away from destroying virtually all life on the planet. It looks so small. If I didn't know what I was looking at, I'd think it was a distant star or perhaps Jupiter.

It's strange that something that's only twenty miles in diameter can extinguish nearly all life on the planet. It hardly seems fair. The meteor that killed off all the dinosaurs was only six miles in diameter. It struck the Yucatan Peninsula in Mexico with a hundred million megatons of force. But it wasn't the initial impact that killed off all the dinosaurs—it was the dust and debris that was released into the atmosphere that was the main culprit. This cataclysmic event caused such dramatic climate change, blotting out the sun for so long, that planets wilted and died, setting off a chain reaction of death up the food chain. The dinosaurs that died off during the initial impact were the lucky ones. Unlike a campy sci-fi film from the nineties, there wasn't a crackpot team of deadbeats and scoundrels with hearts of gold to rocket into space with a nuclear payload to destroy the thing. The world's foremost astrophysicist, Dr. Howard Faulk, and former college roommate of the United Nations Secretary-General Vivek Kumar, explained that even if we managed to intercept the hunk of rock and ice, detonating a nuclear weapon wouldn't vaporize it. It would only blow it apart, and the smaller chunks would still be large enough to pummel the planet with the force of a thousand nuclear warheads. So the decision was made to do nothing. What was the point? Apparently there wasn't one.

As I stare into the heavens and gaze upon the face of the object that's going to kill me, I'm thankful that the asteroid is going to strike somewhere in the Mojave Desert. Only living fifty miles from there, the force of the impact will be so strong that anything within a hundred-mile radius will be incinerated. That's why Southern California is a virtual ghost town. People with means to leave did weeks ago. I don't get it. These people are just prolonging the inevitable.

"Hey," a voice says.

I sit up with a start. Jude sits next to me. "Holy crap! You scared the hell out of me. How long have you been sitting there?" I say, my heart pounding in my chest.

"Just got here," he says, pushing his hair away from his face. "I climbed up the rain gutter."

"What are you? A ninja?"

He stares up at the sky. "It's beautiful, isn't it?" he says. "It's strange how many things that are beautiful can inflict so much pain and death."

"Jude, where's your family?" I ask.

"I don't have any. Not anymore."

"What happened?"

He shrugs, and says, "Time."

I wait for him to continue, but he doesn't. "Time?"

"The greatest force of change in the universe is time," he says. "With enough time a single man could level a mountain." He gets up, dusts off his pants, and heads to the edge of the roof. He lowers himself down the rain gutter and disappears from sight.

Lying in bed that night, I listen to the sound of meteors crashing into the ground echo like distant thunder. I fall asleep to the lulling sound of death and destruction.

The asteroid will strike the Earth today. I'm surprised that I'm not filled with dread. I just want it to be over with. I'm tired of living with this thing, this death sentence, something I'm unable to change.

My father lies sprawled asleep on the floor, lying amongst family photos that look like the rubble of our lives. This might be the first sleep he's had in days, so I leave him there, lightly snoring.

I step outside and look toward the sky. While I'd been preparing for this day for the last couple of weeks, nothing could've prepared me for what I see. There isn't a cloud in the sky, but the dull grey shadow that is cast over the neighbourhood is from the sun being blotted out of the sky by the mountain that hurtles right toward us. It looks like I can reach out and touch it, like those cold winter nights when the full moon looks like it hangs just a few miles overhead. I'm unable to look away. It's like passing a deadly accident on the freeway and finding it impossible not to gawk.

I don't know how long I stare at it. I only look away when I feel the presence of someone near me. Jude hovers nearby and gives me a sad smile. He takes a seat on the grass. He glances up at the asteroid. "How much time do you think we have?"

"I don't know. Ten or fifteen minutes."

I look to the house, hoping my father is awake and standing at the back door, but he's not. He's sound asleep on the photographs. I consider running in and waking him up, but then I figure that it would probably be best just to let him sleep through it. Isn't that everyone's dream to die peacefully while asleep? I don't know how peaceful it will be to be incinerated by the impact of the space rock, but if he's asleep he won't know the difference.

"Tell me something you've never told another living person," Jude says. I study his face and find nothing but sadness and sorrow. It's like he's stuck out in the middle of the ocean, treading water, and desperately wanting someone to throw him a life preserver.

"I blame myself for my mother's death," I say. "The only reason she was driving that day was to come and pick me up from school. I pretended to be sick to get out of having to take a math test I didn't study for. If it wasn't for me, she wouldn't have been driving through the Bristol intersection right at the moment a car ran a red light, killing her."

There's a deafening boom directly overhead. The meteor is consumed in flames as it enters the atmosphere. Jude jumps to his feet and pulls me close. We stare at the enormous ball of flames plummeting toward us. Before I know what's happening, he kisses me on the mouth. When he pulls back, he glances toward the sky. He closes his eyes and . . .

He is suddenly in front of me. His hands touch my face. Tears well up in Jude's eyes, eyes that are glassy and unfocused, eyes that seem to scream at the top of their lungs . . .

Before I know what's happening, someone holds me tightly, their face nuzzled into my neck. I push back from the person and realize that it's Jude. "What's going on?" I say. He drops to his knees and looks up at me. I barely recognize him. He wears a mask of desperation and his clothes are tattered and filthy. I glance up at the sky and see the flaming asteroid falling toward us. It looks different . . .

I'm suddenly lying on the ground with my arms wrapped around him. He howls, and it sounds more like an animal than human. "Jude, are you—" What I was going to say is forgotten as I gaze toward the sky. The asteroid has changed. Even its shadow is smaller. It can't be my imagination. The asteroid is getting . . .

In a blink of an eye, I'm no longer in my backyard. I'm standing on the roof of the mall parking structure. I look in the direction of my house right as something falls from the sky. From this vantage point, I can't see where it hit, but a few seconds later, I hear the sound of an impact. The ground rumbles and a series of car alarms are set off.

I'm lightheaded and I reach out for the guardrail to brace myself. A wave of nausea crashes down on me. I breathe deeply in through my nose and out through my mouth, desperately trying to not throw up. I look up into the sky and see nothing but blue skies. My nausea momentarily forgotten, I spin around and look for the asteroid. But it's not there. It's gone.

I run to the stairs and take them three at a time as I make my way to the ground floor. Racing down the sidewalk, I pass people who filter out into the street. Everyone is looking up. Many people embrace each other. I hear words like "miracle," "saved," "divine." They point toward the sky and yell that we're safe. The asteroid is gone.

I keep running as fast as I can. My lungs burn, but I push myself on. It's like I'm being pulled toward home. Making my way down my street, I race across the front yard. I swing open the front door and find my father still asleep on a bed of photographs in the front room. "Dad! Dad, wake up!" I say, bending down to shake him. "Something has happened!"

His eyelids flutter and finally open.

"It's gone."

He sits up and rubs his eyes. "What's gone?"

"The asteroid," I say.

He studies my face. "What're you talking about?"

I jump to my feet and extend my hand to him. "I'll show you." He takes my hand as he gets up. We rush out to the backyard. I survey the sky, slightly fearful that the asteroid will be up there, and it was just a figment of my imagination that we were saved. But it's not there, and we are saved. "See," I say. "It's gone."

When my father doesn't respond, I turn to him. Instead of staring up, he's looking down at the ground in our backyard at a gaping, smouldering crater. It's about the size of a swimming pool, and a rock the size of a basketball rests at the bottom. The rock is charred and scorched and smoke rises off it, drifting lazily into the air where it dissipates in the warm spring breeze, disappearing from sight like it was never there.

"How's it possible?" he mumbles.

In the coming weeks, that's the question leading scientists attempt to answer. How was it possible that the giant asteroid, which was the size of an island, be whittled down to a rock the size of a large ball? Even accounting for the 3,000 degree temperature reached during entering the atmosphere, there's no possible way that much of the asteroid's mass would've burned up, leaving behind a mere fraction that caused the crater in our backyard.

It took a while for the world to begin operating in a normal fashion. Billions of people awoke from a nightmare, but it seemed to be difficult for them to shake it off completely. It was as if the world had been frozen leading up to the fateful day, and it took a while to thaw. Soon the world picked itself up, dusted off, and started moving again. People who'd waited to die, had to learn to live again. It was a slow process, and people have speculated that it will take years to get back to what the world was like before learning of the asteroid.

I looked for Jude, but he'd disappeared. I couldn't find him next door. There was no trace of him. It didn't take long before the Griffith family reclaimed their home and resumed their lives. They were shocked when I'd told them about the mysterious squatter who'd vanished. Nothing was out of place, and the house was as they left it.

To catch up for lost time, school started up in June with the intention of going through the summer and rolling into the fall with no break. With the exception of the summer temperatures, everything was back to normal. I was forced to get up early for cheerleading practice, senior prom was to be held right after July Fourth and teenagers once again went back to thinking of themselves as indestructible.

I try my hardest to slip back into a normal groove, but the events of that day are hard to put behind me. The images of Jude are seared into my memory, and I can't shake them. With each jarring image of him, his mental state seemed to unravel. I tried to make sense of how I suddenly found myself on top of the parking garage, but I just didn't have a reasonable explanation. On a pecking order of strange things that happened that day, what happened to me didn't command much attention. A world-killing asteroid virtually disappeared. I tried to not dwell on Jude and push those strange events out of my mind.

Getting up late on a Saturday morning, I find my father shaved, showered and dressed for the day. He sits on the floor and rips open the cellophane wrap on a photo album. He opens it and begins putting photos into the sleeves.

"Wow, look at you," I say. "Do you have a hot date or something?"

He grins. "Thought I'd do a test run for Monday."

"What's Monday?"

"I'm going back to work," he says, picking up the photo of my mother lying in a hospital bed holding me when I was a newborn. He looks at the photo and then carefully slides it into the album sleeve.

The doorbell rings.

Two men stand on our doorstep, one with glasses and clutching a clipboard, and another in a military uniform with a gun holstered on his belt.

"Hello," I say.

"Good morning," says the man with glasses. "You must be Brenda Alonso."

"Yeah."

He extends a hand, and says, "I'm Howard Faulk."

I shake his hand. "Hey, I know you. You're that astrophysicist that told us we were toast. Right?"

He chuckles as he adjusts the glasses on his nose. "Yes, that's me. And boy, oh boy, am I glad that I was wrong. My colleague, Captain Rob Denton, and I would like to take a look around your property."

"What can I help you with?" my father says, approaching the door.

"We'd like to look at the meteor in your backyard."

My father looks at the man in uniform, his eyes lingering on the gun. He motions to the side of the house. "You can go around the side."

"Thank you," the man says.

"We'll also need to ask your daughter some questions," the uniformed man says.

"What about?" my father says.

"That's classified."

My father wraps his arm around my shoulders. "I don't know what this is—"

Captain Denton takes a step toward us. "This is a matter of national security."

"I don't care," my father says. "I'm not going to let my daughter—"

"We can do this the hard way or the easy way," he says. "It's totally up to you."

The uniformed man and my father hold each other's stare, as if locked in a war of wills. Howard raises his hands in mock surrender. "Gentlemen, there's no need for this. Brenda, will you show me the backyard?"

"Sure," I say, stepping outside. He follows behind me. As I unlatch it, I see that Captain Denton and my father glumly follow behind us. Swinging the gate open, we walk along the side of the house to the backyard. I motion to the crater. "There it is."

Howard clutches the clipboard to his chest and gawks at it. "Oh, my. Isn't that a beauty?" With his smart phone, he snaps photo after photo from every angle. "Has this remained undisturbed since it was pushed from the sky?"

"Pushed?" I say.

Howard glances at the captain, whose stare is cold and hard.

"Since it fell from the sky?"

"Yes," I say.

Howard goes to the lip of the crater and scoots down on his butt. He dusts himself off and inspects the meteor closely, moving around it, bending down and nearly putting his cheek against the bottom of the crater.

"Is it there?" Captain Denton asks.

"I don't see it."

"See what?" I ask.

Either not hearing the question or just ignoring it, the military man pulls a satellite phone from inside his jacket, dials a number, and speaks into it: "We're going to need an extraction team for the meteor."

Howard pulls a pen from his pocket and touches its tip to the meteor. Smiling, he looks up at the uniformed man. "There appears to be . . . chisel marks."

"Are you sure?"

Howard nods his head, "Yeah. He was telling the truth."

"Who was telling the truth?" my father says, his voice strained.

"That's classified," the captain says.

My father gets in the military man's face. "I've had just about enough of this. Either you—"

"Jude," I say to myself. It's not until Howard looks at me do I realize that I said it out loud.

"You know, don't you?" Howard says, scrambling out of the crater. "What can you tell me about him?"

"I don't know," I say.

"Is this the boy who was squatting in the house next door?" my father asks.

A firm hand grabs my wrist and squeezes. "Tell us what you know?" Captain Denton says.

Startled, I yelp, and pull my arm away from him.

"Get your hands off my daughter," my father says, pushing us apart.

The soldier rests his hand on the butt of his revolver. "You're interfering with a government investigation."

My father motions to the man's hand on the gun. "Are you kidding me with this? You come to our house and threaten me and my daughter."

Howard puts his hands up, and says, "Will everyone please calm down? This isn't helping anything."

"Then tell Sergeant Slayer over here to back the hell off," my father says.

"Would you mind if I talk to your daughter privately?" Howard says.

"What about?"

"About this Jude Simon."

My father looks at me. I shrug. "For just a minute."

Howard motions for me to follow him, and we walk to the front yard. He motions to the house next door. "Is that the house your father was talking about? The one Jude stayed at?"

"Yeah."

Howard stares at the house. "How long was he there?"

"I don't know for sure," I say. "It was after you gave that press conference, and the Griffiths left to be with family. So it was early April I suppose."

He stares at the house, as if trying to piece together a puzzle, but he hasn't figured out how it fits. "Do you know why he picked that house?" When I don't answer he looks at me. His stare is heavy, as if it carries weight, and it presses down on my chest and makes it hard to breathe. I shake my head. A smile spreads across his face. "He doesn't talk much, but when he does, he speaks about you."

"What?"

"It's true," he says. "He mostly babbles, speaking gibberish, but in his lucid moments he speaks of Brenda. It's then that he seems most at peace."

"Jude's alive?"

Howard nods his head.

"Where is he?"

He glances toward the backyard, and when he speaks, it's in a hushed tone. "He's at Camp Pendleton. Not far from here."

"Can I see him?"

Howard shakes his head. "I'm afraid that's not possible. At least not now."

My voice goes up two octaves when I say, "Why not? I need to see him. I've—"

He puts a finger to his lips, pleading with me to lower my voice. "He's been deemed a national security risk."

"What's going to happen to him?"

"I don't know," he says. "I wouldn't worry about it. When he wants to, he can just walk out of there. Nobody can hold him against his will."

"I don't understand," I say.

He studies my face for a moment. "You don't know, do you?"

"Know what?"

"Jude is an extratemporal," Howard says. "He is not tethered to the confines of time." My expression must convey my complete and utter lack of understanding. He might as well be speaking another language. "The way you and I are affected by time is like being on a moving sidewalk at an airport. We continually move forward. That's the only direction through time that we can travel. Jude can walk backwards, or run forwards, or even manipulate the conveyor belt to stop for everyone else, but he can maneuver around while time is frozen." Howard looks around to make sure nobody is listening. "Jude suffered severe psychological trauma, and he's not entirely coherent, so we're doing our best to piece together how he did it. How he destroyed the asteroid. It must've taken him hundreds of years. Maybe a thousand. He did it all while we were frozen in time. Can you imagine? All that time alone, nobody he could talk to. No wonder he lost his mind."

"I . . . I can't . . . believe it," I mutter.

"When I was a child, my father told me that a photograph of my mother kept him going when he was in the trenches during World War II. I believe that's what you did for Jude. When he was about ready to give up, he'd visit you and he vowed to fight on."

I don't know how long I stand there, lost in the moment, seconds feeling like hours.

Shielding my eyes with my hand, I gaze up at the sky. "How did he get up there?"

Howard chuckles. "I don't know. I keep asking him, but he's not making sense right now. I can't even imagine how he did it. I guess if you have enough time, anything is possible."

It doesn't take long before a convoy of military vehicles line our residential street. Men in fatigues remove the fence from the side of our house to accommodate the large truck with the lift. My father and I watch as the soldiers carefully attach a harness to the meteor. Once it's securely fastened, the lift on the truck revs and slowly hoists the rock from its resting spot at the bottom of the crater.

My father drapes his arm around my shoulder and pulls me in close. We watch as the rock dangles above the hole. Something at the bottom of the rock catches my attention. I squint and strain to get a better look, but it sways and spins in the harness. I push my way through the dozen or so soldiers to the edge of the crater.

One of the men barks, "Stand back!"

Not listening, I slide down to the bottom of the crater. I look up at the dangling meteor, and it's clearly visible between an exposed portion of the harness. It's uneven and sloppy, like a bored inmate chiseling a girlfriend's name into the stone wall of his cell. But there's no mistaking it.

Brenda.

Unraveled Hearts

Diane Dubas

It was dangerous but anything worth doing usually is. I watched Cinder crawl through the hole at the bottom of the chain-link fence surrounding the school. The air was dark and sticky with late-summer humidity, smelling of fresh-cut grass and dirt. She'd promised me a good time, promised that tonight would be something I would never forget. If she were any other girl I would have thought she planned some sordid make-out session under the stars, but Cinder was not just any girl. The light caught the edges of her hair and she smiled at me, widely, freely.

"Are you coming?"

There are times when you should just run away. This might have been one of those times. I glanced over my shoulder and then back to Cinder. She'd moved flush with the fence, her dark fingers looped through the chain links, her smile small and mocking.

"Are you scared?" she whispered.

A shiver went down my spine and I drew in a quick breath.

"I'm not scared of anything."

"Liar."

She laughed and gave me that look. It was the same look that she'd hooked me with, a lazy, smug half-smile and hooded eyes, like she was daring me to run away. Like she'd be disappointed if I did. I ducked down and climbed under the fence.

It was always like this with Cinder—I always felt like I had to push the boundaries of everyday life just to keep her interested. My mom didn't like her, of course, and before we'd come out here, we'd been in my room. On my bed, more specifically. Cinder kissed like it was her last night on earth, every night. It's so easy to get lost in her, so easy to get swept up in her wild ideas. Mom kicked her out at ten and then I'd gone back up to my room, climbed out the window and fell into my mother's prized hosta plant. My ankle still hurt, but Cinder's daring grin was worth the pain.

Cinder's hand was warm as she helped me up. I stared at her fingers interlocked with mine. They were stained blue-black from the tips of her fingers and fading around her first knuckles. If you could see her hands, you might think she's an artist, or maybe an overzealous car mechanic. You might wonder about the staining and where it came from. But the thing is: you can't see the stains. No one can. At least no one normal. Oh man, I wish I was normal.

I watched her fingers separate from mine, felt them in my hair, under my chin, and then I was looking at her face. Her eyes reminded me of the perfect cup of coffee—deep, warm, safe. Her lips were hot against mine. It was times like this that I forgot about the danger of being with her. We broke apart and her face split readily into that daring grin again.

"Let's go," she said, pulling me down the hill and into the football field.

We stopped in the middle of the field; the sounds of cars rushing up and down Drummond Road and Lundy's Lane were muted down here as though we'd entered some secret, sound-proofed valley in the middle of the city.

"This is perfect," she said.

She pulled a bag out of her jacket pocket and before it even unrolled, I knew what it contained.

"Cinder, I don't think—"

"See, that's your problem," she said, reaching into the bag and pulling out a handful of long, tapered white candles, "You think too much."

She handed me a candle and then started setting up a circular perimeter around me.

"Cinder, I don't think this is a good idea."

She ignored me and continued with her set up, lighting the candles and surrounding us in a ring of light. After she lit the last candle, she walked back to me, smiling. Like always, I felt instantly protected, like nothing could touch me, us. Like this ill-advised rendezvous was totally legit.

"All you have to do is light the candle, Al."

Sure, all I have to do is light a candle. What's the big deal? If she'd meant lighting the candle *traditionally,* then there was no big deal. But that's not what she meant. I watched her hands as they came away from me and dropped to her sides. Her fingers looked black in the orange glow of the candlelight. Those stains I was talking about? Those are clear evidence that nothing about Cinder is traditional. Magic stains. It turns the fingers of its users a really deep blue, almost black. The more you use, the worse the staining. My fingers are untouched by magic, pale and pink.

For as long as I can remember, I've been able to see things that other people can't. The stains are a perfect example, although admittedly I've only seen them a few times. The first time I saw the stains was when my parents took me to a carnival when I was little. We saw a woman who could read a crystal ball. I had watched her hands as they danced around the crystal, mesmerized by the deep blue stains on her fingertips. I asked my mom about her blue fingers, but she had no idea what I was talking about and had dragged me away to forget with cotton candy and carnival rides. The next time I saw them was in eighth grade when Mary-Anne McDonald told me she had tried to cast a love spell on Matt Roche. Her fingers had held the slightest tint of blue.

I don't remember when I put it together that the blue stains had to do with magic, but somehow I knew. It was almost like I had always known in the same way that you know that white hair has to do with growing old. The stains, however, are the least of my problems. My real problem lies with the threads, the ribbons, the ropes. I can see them: dangling untethered, tied tightly. Where there is magic, there is a thread of some kind, and for some reason, I can see them. Worse,

I can touch them. And when I do, it ends in disaster.

"Cinder," I started.

"Alice, you need to stop being afraid of what you can do."

"You don't know that I can do anything!"

"Of course you can! Why else can you see it?"

Her face was hopeful, excited. I knew that she wanted to share this with someone but she didn't get it. I don't want this. I never wanted to use magic.

"Maybe that's all I can do."

"Maybe it's not."

The thing is, Cinder isn't exactly wrong. Seeing the staining, which is apparently not common amongst magic users, is not the only thing I can do. She just doesn't know what else I can do; she doesn't know what happens when I touch the threads and ribbons that I can see.

The only time I'd reached out and pulled on one, Carrie van Husem ended up in the hospital. I was six. The thread was just hanging off her dress, shimmering in the summer sunlight. I'd seen my mom pull loose threads off my clothes before, pull and tear. I thought I was helping Carrie. I thought I was doing a good thing. I reached out my pudgy little arm and yanked on the thread. It's difficult to describe exactly what happened then, but Carrie seemed to be lifted from the ground, spinning through the air. She'd landed in the middle of a hedge. Things definitely could have been worse, but when it happened, her grandmother came out, speaking in a different language, making the sign of the cross, pushing me off their property. I stopped acknowledging the threads after the Carrie incident. In fact, I studiously ignored them. I went on a personal crusade to completely close my eyes to *all* magic.

That is until I met Lia "Cinder" Evans.

The first time I saw Cinder was at Rachel's party last year. She was cute in this bohemian musician kind of way with her dreadlocks and piercings. She had a kind face and a quick smile. She looked *fun;* she *embodied* fun.

And then I'd seen her hands.

I should have left the party, but instead I stood there staring at her hands. When she finally noticed and narrowed her eyes at me, I forced myself to turn away and fight my way outside of the house. I remember that moment vividly. The air was thick with humidity and Karen Petrovski was puking in the hydrangea bush on Rachel's front lawn. I had started walking down the driveway with no clear thought in my head other than the sight of that girl's hands and her blue fingers. I'd never seen staining so intense. I didn't really know what it meant, except that it was trouble. She was trouble. And then, there she was, Trouble, loping along beside me.

"Hey, do you use?"

Those were her first words to me. The sticky night air clung to my skin as I paused and stared at the strange girl who had walked up beside me. She held up her hands and I couldn't help but stare at her indigo fingertips.

"I don't know what you're talking about," I said, still staring at her hands.

She'd frowned at me then, a sort of thoughtful grimace, and then looked at her hands.

"I think you do."

"No, I don't. I don't even know who you are."

She frowned at me again, a deeper, even more thoughtful grimace. I hadn't liked the way she'd seemingly cornered me in the wide-open like this and Karen's retching was really starting to get to me, so I started walking again.

Cinder hadn't bothered to follow me, but she said instead, "I'm talking about magic, Princess."

Well, that had given me pause. She was the first person to say it. To really say it to me. Magic. Bam. I wasn't crazy. Someone else could see it, too. I stopped and turned around quickly.

"What?"

"What do you see on my hands?"

I stared at the strange girl with her wild dreads and her labret piercing, gleaming in the moonlight. I don't know how long we stood there, just staring at each other, locked in an eyeball battle of the soul. Then I took a leap. Why, I'll never know. Maybe it had just been morbid curiosity. But I took it, anyway.

"Your fingers are stained," I whispered.

I didn't think she'd heard me, but then her face lit up with a wide grin. I don't think I've ever seen anyone more beautiful than Cinder was in that moment. All her hard edges were softened; her eyes held a bright wonder. *I* had done that by talking about *magic*, of all things. Suddenly I felt like I had made a wise decision. That this strange and striking girl would help me figure out all the things I didn't have answers for. That I had a kindred spirit in the world and that she was actually standing in front of me.

The next time I saw Cinder, she was sitting on the bleachers by the football field. She didn't even go to Myer. It was second period. I still don't know how she knew that I had P.E.—knowing her, she'd probably hacked the school's computers and downloaded my schedule. I had never been more aware of someone watching me in my life as I had been that muggy September morning, running a very slow "Marauder Mile" around the football field.

Every time I passed by, her deep blue fingers caught my eye. She scared me, to be honest. She knew something about me that no one else knew and it hadn't scared her. And there was more to it, too. Always, always there was more to it. I liked her. That honestly scared me more than the magic. I had liked other girls, but not like this. Not in a way that was almost tangible. The way she looked at me— not like I was just another friend, but like I was *special*—made my heart pound.

I waited, taking my time pretending to tie my shoe and letting my classmates filter into the building. Cinder had stayed on the bleachers, watching me. Then I'd straightened my shoulders and walked to the base of the bleachers, lifting my chin defiantly.

"What are you doing here?" I asked her.

That slow, steady grin of hers grew as she considered my question. "I'm here for you, Princess."

She hopped down the bleachers in fluid, arcing movements. Parkour, she told me later, was the wave of the future. Tomorrow's choice of transport. Cinder was taller than me, somehow intimidating in her surplus army jacket and wide-legged jeans, me in my white gym shirt and ugly purple sweat shorts. I hugged myself as though it would protect me from the very potential of rejection.

"Because of magic," I said, my voice dwindling into a whisper.

Cinder shrugged, never taking her eyes off my face. "Because you're magic."

It was like a romantic comedy the way my breath caught; the stupid little gasp I made.

"Get changed, I want to show you something," she said. It wasn't really a request.

"But, I have Physics," I mumbled uselessly.

"So? Physics hasn't changed in the last four and a half billion years. The earth still spins, gravity's still nine point eight meters per second squared, ticker tape has no expiry," she said flippantly.

It was easy to smile. Cinder always makes everything so easy. It was easy to skip class—something I *never* did. It was easy to follow her to the bus, to let her take me to the woods. It was so easy. Then she showed me how easy it was for her to start fires from nothing. Not nothing—with *magic*. Of course I could see it all happen. It was fascinating because I didn't know how to make anything with magic, only how to take it all apart.

We talked for hours in that dark alcove of trees. She told me what she knew and I told her about the stains, the threads, and that I didn't know what I was doing. Cinder told me that there were others—people on the internet, all over the world, who could do what she could. She hadn't heard of anyone who could do what I could do, but Cinder never despaired. She was sure it was just a matter of finding the right contact online.

My courage disappeared with the sun and when it started to get dark, I told her that I had to go home. I practically ran from her because she represented everything I had been avoiding and everything I was afraid of doing. Magic, but also her. I didn't really hear her following me out of the woods and I jumped when her cold fingers circled my wrist gently.

"Al," she said, already taking liberties with my name.

My eyes met hers and I knew I was lost. Even that early in the game, I was lost. I thought it would be yet another experience with unrequited feelings. Another girl who just wanted to be friends. It was like she could read my mind, trapping me with deep brown eyes that betrayed a warm heart under all that bluster. I tensed when she kissed me, surprised that it had happened, worried that I was dreaming. When we broke apart, I recognized something in her that I'd never associated with Cinder. It was just a flicker, but it was there in the nervous way she bit her bottom lip. She'd been *hoping*, too.

I never really stopped hoping with Cinder.

But that all lead to *there*—to standing in that field, surrounded by candles and faced with a terrifying and likely impossible task. I looked past her at the candles lined up around us, each with a gently flickering flame and if I stared hard enough, I could see it—the thread extending from each flame, tiny and wavering, like a hair dancing in the wind. Cinder knows how to manipulate those threads, how to push down the physical flames and pull the threads into place as she wants them. She's pretty good at it now. But Cinder does not see the threads. And in all the time I've known Cinder, I've never once heard her speak of anyone who can, so I just never brought it up again after the first time. It's bad enough that she'd never heard of the staining before.

"If I do this, will you stop bothering me about it?"

Cinder grinned. "Absolutely."

I raised an eyebrow. "Really?"

"For now."

"Cinder."

"Alice," she said, using my tone to mock me. "Just do it. Nothing is going to happen."

"Where have I heard that before?"

"We're in the middle of a field! The only thing that could happen right now is that some nosy old woman sees the lights and calls the cops, so hurry up."

I turned what I felt was an impressive glare on her but she only laughed in response. This isn't the first time she'd tried to get me to use magic. She tried all the time. Generally she would whittle me down with kisses and sweet words, lowering my defences and sneaking it in. Tonight she was taking a different approach—a direct approach. No kisses and sweet words, just magic and silently issued dares.

I looked again at the threads dancing in the flames and then closed my eyes. I tried to imagine physically plucking each thread and connecting it to the wick of my candle. I opened my eyes. The candle in my hand was decidedly unlit.

"It didn't work."

"You didn't even try!"

"I did!"

"Lame. Look, you have to actually reach out and *feel* it."

She pulled a candle out of her pocket and I watched as she focused her energy on the wick. I could see, too, a ball of *Cinder* surrounding her body. The ball seemed to stretch out and touch each of the candles, neatly snipping off a tiny fragment of each of the threads and re-aligning them with the unlit wick. The candle in her hand lit up with a bright flare and then eased back to a smaller flame.

"See? Easy."

Easy, she said. The thing was I'd tried to reach out with my mind like that, to release a bubble of *Alice*, but it never worked. The only time I've ever been able to do anything like that is when someone hurts me. And then it's scary and I have no control over it, then it's twice the size of what Cinder can do.

In seventh grade, Nick Valenti shoved me down the stairs at school—I was fine, miraculously unharmed, but Nick . . . He'd ended up slammed into the wall at the top of the stairs and suffering a concussion that kept him out of school for days. He claimed I had somehow pushed him back but anyone who saw what happened said I was already falling down the stairs when Nick slammed into the wall. He'd called me a witch and some other, less-pleasant names, and essentially made the next two years of my life hell. That wouldn't have been such a big deal if he was just another bully and I was just another victim. But Nick was a victim, too. A victim of magic I couldn't even control.

Cinder can't see this either, the ball of energy she produces. She had looked at me like I was insane when I'd asked her about it. Cinder has no idea what I can do; what I can see.

I tried to focus my energy again, but nothing happened. The threads danced before me. I knew I could just reach out and snatch one physically, but I wouldn't know what to do with it next. When I'd grabbed a thread in the past, the magic just *fell apart*. And someone got hurt. It wasn't worth it.

"Come on, Alice. I know you can do this."

That look was on her face again—half dare, half threatened disappointment. I hated that look. I hated how it made me feel. I hated to be a disappointment to anyone. I stared at the wick, avoiding her eyes, and that's when it happened. I was thinking about how I wanted to do this just to prove to Cinder that I could, just so she wouldn't be disappointed in me, just so I wouldn't lose her. Ever since meeting her, I'd felt like I wasn't alone anymore, like there was hope for me after all. Maybe I didn't feel like I wasn't a freak, but I did feel like I wasn't the only freak. I didn't want to lose that. Then it came, that bubble of *me*, and I saw it surrounding us, I saw the candles flicker and flutter and threaten to go out. The threads of the flames, though, seemed to grow and become thicker, stronger.

I laughed as the threads grew longer and then I saw Cinder's face. She was saying something, but I couldn't hear her. All I could hear was the blood rushing through my veins, my heart pounding against my chest. I panicked when I realized that I didn't have control over it, that the candle in my hand was burning, the flame growing, bursting, flaring upwards and sideways—a bright blaze in the darkness. I dropped it to the ground when the scalding wax hit my hands. My panic only seemed to make the ball bigger and more irregular. I didn't know how to pull it back in. My eyes found Cinder's and I knew that I was in serious trouble. She was afraid, I could see it on her face, and she was pushing through the energy surrounding me. Then there was one split second where I could hear her voice, her arms wrapped tightly around me, warm and safe.

"Alice, breathe with me," she seemed to whisper. She later told me she was screaming it in my ear.

I inhaled when she did, exhaled when she did. My focus shifted to her, slowly and surely, and I felt the power shakily return to wherever it had come from. She released me carefully and stepped back, her hands still on my arms. I expected the fear to still be present in her face, but instead her smile was huge, her eyes were enormous, and even with sweat streaming down her face, she looked energized.

"See? Easy."

I started to laugh and then I felt it, a burst of magic that hadn't dissipated. I watched, as if in slow motion, as it stretched out and hit Cinder in the chest. She flew up into the air and backward, arms and legs flailing forward as she went. It would have been comical if it wasn't so frightening. She hit the ground with a dull crack, her leg splayed out at a funny angle. My body took forever to function, my legs refusing to work, but then they did and I was beside her. She was silent, unconscious.

"Cinder? Cin? Lia! Lia, wake up!"

My voice was high-pitched, frantic as I reached out to shake her. She wouldn't wake up and her leg was still stuck at that weird angle. I don't know how long I sat there, crying desperately at Cinder to wake up. Everything that followed was a blur.

❧

I hadn't seen Cinder in three weeks. I hadn't answered her calls or texts or emails. I hadn't responded to any of her attempts to speak to me. It hadn't been easy, not when she was throwing stones at my bedroom window and texting me every ten minutes to annoy me into responding. She wasn't annoying me though. Every stone clattered against my unraveling heart; every text was answered with tears. I'd been hoping that she would get the hint and leave me alone. I was hoping to avoid this. How do you break up with the one person who really understands you? The person who makes you glad to be alive. And how was I going to stand in front of her and tell her no. Cinder doesn't take no as an answer. Cinder will fight for me, even as I'm running like a coward.

My eyes scanned over the last text one more time.

Meet me at S at 10. Don't be late and don't be lame.

I don't know what had possessed me to come here. Maybe if she saw me, she would see the resolution in my eyes. I wasn't going to back down from this. We were over and there would be no changing that. My fingers curled around the phone tightly as I reached for the door handle. Finishing this would be the only way to move on, no matter how hard it would be to see her. I climbed out of the car. This is where it had happened, here. And there she was, standing in the middle of that scorched circle we'd left behind that night. If we were caught here, we'd both be doing time in juvie.

Cinder's back was to me, her tall, curvaceous figure shortened as she leaned against her crutches. I stopped in my tracks. What was I even doing? Last time we'd been together, I'd, well, I'd hurt her. It had been my fault. The general message I'd gotten through her emails and texts and voicemails was that she didn't blame me, if anything she blamed herself. I considered turning and running, but then Cinder spoke.

"You're late."

I couldn't think of anything to say. It was hard to believe that just three weeks ago, I would have had a smart reply. We would have joked and laughed. She would have convinced me that the world was right with warm kisses and soft touches. But that was then and this is now. We had made mistakes; dabbled in things we shouldn't have. Dark things. Things I couldn't control.

Moonlight glinted off her eyes and her shadow was long and impressive, snaking toward me. Her leg had been broken in three places, all the way down. She would need a lot of physio and she might never walk properly again. We'd told everyone—our moms, the police, anyone who asked—that it had been a fall. That we'd been fooling around and Cinder had just tripped and fallen funny. They seemed to just accept that. Cinder's mom had basically rolled her eyes as though this sort of thing was only to be expected, as though

Cinder had a reputation for school suspensions and injuries. The candles and the scorched grass? Well, that had been harder to explain away. We'd both been ordered to stay away from Stamford after school hours; Cinder had been suspended, not that she minded— she didn't really like school anyway. She said that her classmates were small-minded sheep living in a consumerist bubble and she would rather lie in bed conversing with actual humans online.

Cinder started to move toward me laboriously and I fought the urge to run. I didn't want to face her. I didn't want to face the evidence of what I had done. I *couldn't* get back together with her, no matter how much I wanted to—clearly I was a danger to us both. But Cinder just smiled at me.

"I wanted to meet with you," she said simply.

I raised my eyebrows at that. "And you thought this would be the best place?"

Her smile deepened as she looked at me. "I know how hard it is for you to face your fears, Al."

I walked past her, toward the school, both feeling horrible for being able to do it and feeling terrible for doing it. I pulled my jacket tight around me and tried to squeeze out the cool autumn air.

"How'd you even get down here?" I asked, refusing to look at her.

"Alice," Cinder said, as she hobbled behind me.

"I broke your leg, Cin," I forced out.

She was next to me again and I could feel her eyes on me. She shrugged in my peripheral vision. "It was an accident."

I laughed in disbelief. "It shouldn't have happened."

"Hey, Al, look at me."

My eyes met hers and I felt my heart ache a little. I'd missed her, I realized. I missed telling her everything. I missed feeling safe. I missed Cinder. I glanced at the long cast on her leg and recalled my mom's voice as she'd told me that they had to put pins in her leg to fix the bones. When I think about that—think about those long, golden legs mangled to the point of needing pins to repair them and that I had been the cause of that . . . It couldn't happen again. I could never be allowed to hurt her again.

"It can't happen again, Lia. We're done." I'd hoped using her actual name would alert her to how serious I actually was about this.

"Hey, Alice, I told you to do it."

"So? That absolves me? I shouldn't have listened to you."

"It's not a big deal."

Her easy voice irritated me. *It's not a big deal.* But it was a huge deal. I'll never forget the sound. The cry of surprised pain, the sick, dull cracking of bone. It had been my fault. It had been my doing. No matter how many times she tries to tell me that it wasn't my fault, I will never, ever forgive myself. Because I knew. I knew how dangerous playing with magic could be. I knew that I didn't know my own strength. And I had been the one who had allowed myself to be convinced that I could harness the power. I should have known better.

If I could break bones without even realizing it, what else could I do? I looked at my fingers in the moonlight. I could see the staining on my fingertips. It was darkest at the very tips. That's where the energy focuses, Cinder and I had discovered. It started as a pin prick of blue-black on the tips of fingers and spread down the more someone used. Cinder's hands were much worse than mine, but she'd been doing this longer than I had. Not just lighting candles in a schoolyard, but more elaborate schemes—controlled fires in garbage bins that baffled the police, light flares that made UFO seekers frenzied, blooming flowers right in front of my eyes in the dead of winter.

"I have to go," I said, choking back a sob, "Don't call me anymore. Don't try to see me. We can't do this anymore. Even the police agree that we shouldn't be together."

"Al." Her voice was pleading, almost desperate, but I just shook my head and did my best to keep the tears at bay.

She grabbed my arm then and swung me into her, surprisingly strong despite her injuries. The touch of her lips against mine was so familiar, so comforting. I could almost believe that everything would be fine if I could just *stay* here, with her. But when I opened my eyes, she was still leaning on that crutch and her leg was still broken. We were still broken. I pulled away and looked into her eyes—warm, coffee brown eyes. *I'd* have to be the strong one this time. *I'd* have to protect her from me.

"We can't," I whispered. "I'm sorry."

And then I just ran. I ran from the girl I'd hurt, the girl I cared about most. I just ran away. Because it's what I've always done when it comes to this, when it comes to magic.

Mr Trenchant's Service
Keely Cutts

Mr Greyfield's house was at the end of a winding street lined with houses that were misshapen and jagged where they'd fallen into sinkholes. His looked mostly intact, if not welcoming, with a tight shut door and boarded-over windows. Kai climbed up the steps and knocked on the door, Mr Trenchant winding his way through her legs looking for a scrap of food or affection.

From inside the house, Kai could hear a shouted apology. "Just be a moment, I'm coming." The swollen door shuddered in its frame. "Don't leave! It'll just be a moment." The door gave with a screech and an older man with white hair and spectacles wiped a hand across his face. His skin was several shades darker than Kai's own brown complexion. "Damn door. I shaved an inch off the frame just this winter and it still fights me every day." He looked her up and down, and frowned at the cat. Kai was aware that her worn tunic and trousers made her look like she was there for charity. She worked hard to keep them clean and her hair in long, neat braids, but she still didn't look like a professional sorcerer. "What do you want? I've got no room for boarders and no jobs for children."

"Mr Greyfield? I'm with Mr Trenchant's Service." She held up his note with the request and address.

He peered at her, unmoving in the doorway. "I believe," his words were stiff, like he spent a lot of time not talking, or maybe only talking to people who read books all day. "The gentleman at the butcher shop who recommended the service spoke of a young man who helped with his problem."

Syned. He'd been gone for two weeks and just the casual reference to him ignited a ball of hurt in her stomach. "My associate," she said, fighting to keep her hands steady at her side and not twist in the fabric of her tunic. In a sinking city where movement saved lives, she fought to stay still and test the measure of the land beneath her feet. "You said it was a mild infestation. I can handle it."

"How old did you say you were?"

The door swung closed just a bit and she worried that she'd lost his business, no matter what age she told him. She had another slip of paper in her pocket with a different address on the other side of the district and there was no guarantee she'd make it before nightfall. "I'm thirteen and I've been doing this for two years. I can help you."

Maybe he believed her, maybe it was an act of pity, but Mr Grey-field nodded and stepped back to allow her into the house.

"Any secret rooms or hidden passages?" Kai asked as she ran a hand along the walls, feeling for where there might be a hiding place instead of water-swollen wood. "If there is, we won't be responsible for re-infestation." No sorcerer, no matter how powerful, could work the same spell on the same object twice. It was the first lesson sorcerers learned. All of Creona, sorcerer or not, knew it well.

When Kai was small, her father used to take her to the main square at the centre of the city, just before the gates of the castle and let her run along the deep grooves of the spell that was supposed to save Creona. She would make herself dizzy trying to follow the looping swirls and she would tire herself out long before she ever traced the whole pattern. Sometimes, when the water was high and the grooves were filled, she'd race paper boats against other children. Her father said it was a fitting end to one of the greatest magical collaborations in their history.

Six hundred years ago, the empire hired the fifteen best sorcerers to cast a spell to keep the city on dry ground. They chiseled into the paving stones of the square for weeks to create the complicated pattern and for many years it seemed the magic worked. But then, twenty years ago, either the sorcerers weren't as good as they promised, or the weight of the city was too much for the spell. Creona started to sink again. The city was abandoned by all but those too poor or too stubborn to leave.

"Nothing's hidden."

"All right." Kai turned and saw Mr Greyfield standing in the centre of the room, his hands dangling at his sides, like he'd be more comfortable holding something. A book, or a quill. He had enough of each scattered through the room, despite what the damp did to them. "That's all. Come back in the morning and your house will be fairy free."

"Are you sure?" His fingers fluttered against the pages of an open book. "Perhaps I should stay."

Kai shook her head. "Come back in the morning. It won't work if you're here."

After a moment's hesitation, Mr Greyfield collected his things and stepped out of the house, helping Kai close the door with a firm shove from outside.

While Mr Trenchant settled down for a nap on a pile of papers, Kai went to work. She made a slow turn through the room, airing out every cupboard, opening every cabinet. Anything that could be opened was a possible hiding place for fairies and had to be exposed or risk ruining her work. Twenty fairies could easily hide in an ink pot if she forgot to unstopper it.

She finished the main room and then moved on to the rest of the house. It helped that Mr Greyfield didn't own much besides books so it was well before sundown when she finished her inspection. She went back to the main room, dug her awl from the box and rolled up the faded rug to expose the wooden floorboards. The magic worked best when set in stone, but the wood was strong enough to hold the spell. She etched long, flowing lines into the hard wood, careful to keep the pattern clean.

The spell for fairy removal was the simplest of all spells and the first one taught to sorcerers. Kai remembered sitting with her father in his workshop—before a sudden shift swallowed the building and her father whole—learning the pattern, his strong hands holding hers as he guided her through the lines. Syned knew a couple more spells because he was three years older, but Kai had only ever hand the chance to learn the first.

She finished the lines and as the sun set and the spell activated, Kai woke Mr Trenchant and set the trapdoor on the box. She picked the most comfortable looking chair and curled up, waiting for the spell to draw the fairies out from their hiding places. Mr Trenchant did the rest.

❦

In the morning, Mr Greyfield came home to a house free of fairies and didn't try to change the price on her. He handed over four copper coins with a smile. "I would very much like to meet your associate and thank him personally. Or perhaps the elusive Mr Trenchant."

Kai cast a quick glance at the cat. Syned thought that if they used Mr Trenchant's name, their customers would be less suspicious of two young people doing sorcerer's work. "We're very busy, but I'll let them know."

With the sun at her back, Kai made her way through abandoned neighbourhoods and passed empty shops. The tailor at the end of Mr Greyfield's street left last summer and the blacksmith down the next alley not long after. Many of the houses were empty, and the few that were still occupied looked in danger of falling apart.

Tracker's shop was the front end of an abandoned bakery, the warm scent of fresh bread long gone. "Little Kai," he said as she walked in through a set of bodyguards by the door. Tracker was behind his desk—a giant bulky thing that he'd dragged three streets over from an accountant's office. He had his feet propped up on the corner and a mug of something steaming in his hand. His hair was unkempt and he had deep circles under both his eyes. Because of the nature of his profession, Kai couldn't tell if he hadn't slept or if he'd been fighting. "What do you have for me this fine morning?"

She heaved the box onto the desk. "Fifty-eight fairies."

"And?"

"And a silver chain." She drew Mr Greyfield's chain from her pocket and slid it across the desk, feeling a churn of regret in her stomach. No matter how closely she watched her cat, he always managed to take something shiny from their jobs. The first few times she noticed, Kai tried to put them back, but he'd just take something else.

Tracker picked up the chain and held it up to the light of the morning sun. "Mr Trenchant has a good eye, as always." He set the chain aside and turned his attention to the fairies. Only trained sorcerers could cast spells, but untrained people could use magical objects. Fairies went for a good price because they could be used in potions and poultices.

While he was occupied examining the fairies, Kai took advantage of his distraction. "Have you heard anything," she drew a breath, steadying herself to say his name out loud. "From Syned?"

"Not a thing." Tracker sat back, the box abandoned on his desk. "I think you'd hear from him before I would. He hasn't tried to contact you, has he?" Something changed in Tracker when he asked the question. He didn't move, but his attention was sharper, his body poised, hidden under his relaxed sprawl.

Kai had spent the last three days looking for Syned in their favourite hiding spots, the broken old buildings they used to dare each other to enter and along the hidden caverns by the canals. Mold and crumbled masonry were all she found. "No." Kai shifted from foot to foot, waiting for the ground to give way beneath her.

"You know, if they find out he's gone—"

She smacked a hand down on the desk, surprising herself and Tracker. "He's not gone." He promised.

Tracker gave her a slow blink.

"He's not gone," she said, quieter this time.

"If the Reverents find out he's not around, there's going to be trouble." He pulled an apple from his pocket, bright and firm. It crunched as he bit into it. "This is no place for an unattached girl."

She didn't want to talk to Tracker anymore, and tapped the box. "Do you want the fairies or not?"

Tracker continued to stare, making an uncomfortable chill run up her arms and across the back of her neck. She'd never been afraid of him before, but then, Syned had been with her. He shifted his focus to the box and the sharpness of his attention drained away. "Two coppers."

"Two?" She wouldn't be able to eat if the price stayed so low. "Last week you paid twice that."

Tracker dropped his feet off the desk and they landed with a loud thud that made Kai jump. "It's the best I can do. Fairies aren't in high demand right now." He pulled a bag from the desk and shook the fairies from the box, tying the bag tightly once they were inside. He crossed the space between them and gave her back the box before he pressed the coins into her palm, his cool fingertips lingering. "Come see me again, little Kai." As she turned, he reached out and drew his fingers down one of her long braids. "We'll see if we can't find you more suitable work."

Unable to speak, Kai scooped up Mr Trenchant and fled. She ran, long after she lost sight of his shop, even as her legs ached and lungs burned with each breath, until she reached her home. The angled building's first floor was sunk below street level and the only access was through a window that used to be on the second floor. She shoved open the window, pushed the box and Mr. Trenchant through and climbed up the pile of loose stones to squeeze inside. Kai slammed the window shut and leaned, panting, against the glass.

At her feet, Mr. Trenchant rubbed his face against her leg, chirping. His fur was soft beneath her fingers and the rumbling of his purr helped calm her. Her hands were shaking, but the cat didn't seem to mind, curling in closer as she slid down the wall to press her knees against her chest. She wished Syned was there waiting for her, so she could shout at him, and shove him, show him how badly he'd scared her. He'd been so confident when he told her his plan to look for a way out of the city that wouldn't cost them the price of the ferry and the bride to cross, or braving the murderous currents of the river. If only she'd been more afraid and asked him not to go.

The house was sinking, but everything was sinking. She didn't know why Syned wanted to find something so quickly. If he was worried about the house, there were plenty of other houses that were in better shape. His plan sounded like such a good idea, but now, Kai couldn't help but imagine him trapped beneath the rubble of a collapsed building, or lost to a swollen canal. So many things could go wrong, but the thought that haunted her was that he'd left on purpose, left her behind because he was tired of taking care of her.

Kai stayed inside the house the rest of the day. Even as the temperature rose, making the rooms steamy and filling her nose with the sour smell of mouldering wood, she stayed away from the windows. Her heart slowed and she stopped trembling, but she couldn't shake the feeling that someone was watching her.

As the afternoon light began to fade, she gathered up Mr Trenchant, whose name was no longer a protection, and ran to her only other appointment for the week. Mr Browbain let her in and she finished his house with ease, collecting her pay in the morning as Mr Trenchant ran off on his own adventure with the rising sun. Across the street, a tall, lanky boy leaned against a house. She'd seen him a few times in Tracker's shop.

He followed her, close and distasteful, like the slick of pitch on water. She felt safest where other people could see her, so she took a longer route back to her neighbourhood. Along the way, she made sure to speak to as many people as she knew, buying vegetables from the old woman who sold the extra from her garden, and an old client of her father's who sold her strips of dried meat at half price.

Near an open square, a crowd gathered around something Kai couldn't see, and she took the opportunity to lose her shadow in the press of bodies. Without his spying gaze, she released her captured fairies in small groups along a canal, watching them flounder for a moment before they fluttered off in search of new damp homes. She wouldn't go back to Tracker.

Kai stopped at the market to pick up as much as she could buy with her few coins, so she wouldn't have to leave her home. "Good morning, Mr Grinfast," she said as she came to the bread vendor. His baskets were mostly empty and the loaves that remained looked hard and crumbled at the edges. She picked three of the likeliest and held them up. "How much?"

He turned his brown, lined face away from her toward one of Tracker's men lounging at the edge of the market. She hadn't noticed him and she clutched her coins tighter in her hand, ready to run. "Sorry, Miss Kai. The price of bread went up. You don't have enough for even one loaf."

"But how do you know how much I—" She let her hand drop as Mr. Grinfast continued to avoid her eyes. "I guess everything will be too expensive?" She gestured to the other stalls; the vendors couldn't quite seem to look at her.

"I'm sorry, Miss Kai."

She wanted Mr Grinfast's food, not his pity. "I understand," she said, not knowing why she wanted to make him feel better, when what she really wanted was to knock over his stand and stomp the crusty loaves of bread to dust.

At the edge of the market, Tracker's man pushed off from his spot and ambled away. As soon as he was gone, Mr Grinfast called out to her. She turned back, breath caught in her throat at the idea that he might help her now that the man was gone. "Maybe you could try one of the markets in another district."

Hope drained out of her so quickly, she felt unsteady. "Right." Different districts all had their own rules. As uncertain as her situation was in Tracker's territory, in another area, she would be completely vulnerable. Around her the vendors looked upset, but none of them offered to help her and she left before they could see her cry.

That night, Kai stretched out under the broken window pane where she could watch the moon rise. Usually, the slow rise would lull her to sleep, but that night every creak of the swollen wood, and snuffling bark of a stray dog pulled her from an uneasy sleep where she dreamt of half-formed shapes reaching for her, catching the ends of her hair as she tried to escape. The house felt looming in the dark without the sounds of Syned's snoring to fill the empty spaces. Mr Trenchant hadn't returned, leaving her without his huffing wheeze and his warm presence curled up behind her knees.

She woke before dawn, staring out the window as the sky bloomed red. Outside, the quiet of the street was disrupted by the sharp, measured footsteps and chanting of the Reverents. The King sent them to Creona to help keep peace and manage food distribution, but mostly they wandered the streets in packs, scooping up orphans to swell their ranks. Last summer, her friend Maeris went with them after her parents were lost to a flooded canal. Kai saw her a few months later, working with the other orphan Penitents in their ash-grey robes to clear the rubble near the Reverent Seat. She was so thin, Kai could see her bones pressed against her skin and when Kai waved to her, Maeris looked back with empty eyes. Kai never saw her again.

The singing grew closer. Kai sat up and moved away from the window as their footsteps slowed and the chanting stopped.

Someone knocked against the wall of the house. "Come out, Miss Kai. The Reverent Order needs you."

They knew her name. Kai clenched her hands so hard her nails cut into the soft skin of her palms, but the pain helped keep her still and quiet until they went away.

"Come now, Miss Kai. There's no need to be shy. Aren't you tired of caring for yourself? We know you're all alone in that big house and it must be so hard to worry about food. It's not good for a girl to be alone in this city. Let us help you." He sounded so sure, so confident, that Kai was tempted to peek her head out the window and ask about terms. It would be nice to let someone else worry for a while. But then she remembered Maeris, wasted and more broken than when her parents died, and she didn't move.

The chanting started up again and the leader knocked on the house. "We'll be back tomorrow, Miss Kai. Our patience will grow thin the longer you resist us."

Long after the chanting faded, Kai stayed still in her spot, afraid it was a trick and they were just waiting for her to show herself. Syned had promised he'd be gone just a few days. He promised they would leave the city together. He promised she wouldn't have to worry. He might be hurt, or he might have left her behind, but she couldn't go on thinking that he was going to come back at any moment and everything was going to be all right. She wanted to tear the room apart, tear the whole house down. What use was magic when the only spell she could work was to draw fairies from their hiding places?

Her arms ached from holding her legs when Kai finally stood. She couldn't stay in the house. Tracker and the Reverents made it clear that her life was going to change and she wanted to be the one to make the decisions. They might find her, but she needed to move to give herself some time to make a real plan.

From a low shelf, she grabbed a bag and began filling it with food and the things she couldn't leave behind. This was the room where her father taught her to read, where she and Syned invented elaborate games made of string and ribbon. The smell of still water and rotting wood had covered the scents of her childhood long ago. When she closed her eyes, though, she could still remember what it was like to be in the house when it had been a home for the three of them. Leaving felt like letting Tracker and the Reverents win, but staying. Staying would be worse.

Packing consumed her as she sorted through her things, those she needed and those memories better left behind. She was so intent that she didn't notice Mr Trenchant until he brushed up against her leg and dropped a dead mouse at her feet. "I was so worried," Kai said as she picked him up, burying her face in his soft fur. "I thought I would have to leave you behind, too." He tolerated her attention for just a minute before he squirmed free and hopped to the ground where he dropped another item from his mouth.

"What's this?" She picked up a gold coin, marred by his tiny teeth marks. "Where did you find this?" She'd never held one in her own hand before, though her father received one once for a difficult spell.

She gripped the coin in her hand, the heavy weight a reminder it was worth more than she could earn in months. With his gift, Mr. Trenchant offered Kai a new choice. Instead of running inside the city, she could pay to cross the river. Outside of Tracker's influence she could go anywhere, do anything. She could go somewhere cold, where the seasons changed, where it snowed, where everything wasn't being pulled into an unforgiving swamp.

If she left, Syned wouldn't know where to find her, and wouldn't be able to follow on his own. There was no guarantee that it would be any better outside the city—she could be snapped up by a Reverent pack as soon as she cleared the river. But she'd stayed still too long, the ground was bound to shift and swallow her whole if she didn't make a move.

The house already felt empty as she kissed the tips of her first three fingers and pressed them to the warped wood of the window frame. She loved the house and her brother. The memories of what their life was before filled all the spaces in her heart and mind, but they weren't enough to keep her safe. She threw her bag over her shoulder, tucked Mr Trenchant under one arm and slipped out of the house.

Contributors

Valerie Hunter is a high school English teacher and a grad student at Vermont College of Fine Art's Writing for Children and Young Adults program. Her stories have appeared in magazines including *Cicada* and *Cricket,* and in the YA anthologies *Cleavage, Real Girls Don't Rust,* and *Brave New Girls.*

K D Callaghan has a BA in Creative Writing which she uses to write copy by day and fantasy at night. While championing diversity in fantasy is her passion, she also loves Leverage, tea, and the Oxford comma. Her work has appeared in *Room* magazine and she currently serves as the Art and Literature editor at *Paper Droids.*

Maria Dones is a junior majoring in Creative Writing at the University of South Florida. When she's not writing, you'll probably find her watching Netflix with her roommates, going to Disney with her boyfriend, or spending time with her family.

Deborah Walker grew up in the most English town in the country, but she soon high-tailed it down to London, where she now lives with her partner, Chris, and her two young children. Find Deborah in the British Museum trawling the past for future inspiration or on her blog: Deborah Walker's Bibliography Her stories have appeared in *Nature's Futures, Cosmos, Daily Science Fiction* and *The Year's Best SF 18* and have been translated into a dozen languages

L Lark is a writer and visual artist living in Portland, Oregon. She fled the world of science to write about ghosts, monsters, and the places beneath our world. Links to her projects and publications may be found at l-lark.com.

Christopher E Long's debut young adult novel, *Hero Worship*, was a Junior Library Guild Selection. His comic book writing has been published by Marvel Comics, IDW Publishing, and Image Comics. Follow him on Twitter @celong1122 and Instagram @ chriselong

Diane Dubas is a fiction writer living in Burlington, Ontario. She has attended the Humber School for Writers and has no previous publications.

Keely Cutts is an MFA candidate at Rosemont College and has work published or forthcoming in *Front Porch Review* and *Crack the Spine*. Originally from Florida, she now lives in suburban Philadelphia with her wife.

www.ingramcontent.com/pod-product-compliance
Lightning Source LLC
Chambersburg PA
CBHW070339130626
46556CB00007B/2936